# DARLING
# CLEMENTINE

*by*

Andrew Klavan

**THE PERMANENT PRESS**
SAG HARBOR, NEW YORK

Fic

Library of Congress Number: 87-061103
International Standard Book Numbers 0-932966-81-0

Manufactured in the United States of America

THE PERMANENT PRESS
RD2 Noyac Road
Sag Harbor, NY 11963

"She has come amorous it is all she has come for
If there had been no hope she would not have come"

Ted Hughes

# One

My cunt, to begin with, is an orchid. A gigantic orchid in a miniature wood. Sometimes. Other times, it is a gap, an abyss, a gaping scar, still bleeding from when the rabbis held me up, helpless, and sawed off my cock and my balls and laughed because they had made me into a girl, and I was screaming in helpless rage. Then, I hate all men, and especially my father and I dream of having my cock back again and having them all tied over chairs in a row before me, and going down the row quite calmly while they all beg for mercy, fucking each one up the ass in turn so the next one has to watch, begging for mercy. But sometimes, my whole body blossoms out of my cunt, and I am entirely an orchid, receptive, but also complicated, the whole world flowing into me passionately and sweetly and running over my hundred different petals and curves and spaces, taking the shape of all my turns. Then men are like the bearers of the world and I love them, love them in an aching, awe-struck and yet haughty way, like the Christ child must have loved the magi when they came to him with gold and frankincense and myrrh—all the gifts of the world—and he was dazzled by all these grand grownups and yet knew it was he, the infant-god, to whom they came. Oh, I love them so much, and the world which they put on the tips of their penises and bring into me so that it can run off my hundred petals, taking my form.

I was in that mood when I married Arthur. Don't get me wrong. I am not one of these modern women you read about in books. They are so detached and wry and rueful.

I have never met one—only read about them in books—
and I am not like them and do not really believe anyone is.
I love Arthur. We have been married for one week, and it
is like waking up every morning and knowing there is
something wonderful and new about your life, and it is
Arthur. He is like a new toy, and I want to play with him
like a doll, set him naked on my lap like a doll, and feed
him and scold him and turn him over and spank him until
his white bottom turns pink, and then stick my finger into
his ass until he bucks and cries out and comes onto my
thigh. Then I want him to become monstrous, to slap me
and say, "Now, you're in for it, Samantha," and turn me
over roughly and take off his belt with a broad, sweeping
motion of his arm (why he is wearing a belt at this point in
the proceedings is something of a mystery, but there you
are) and run his cock up me like a flagpole, slashing and
slashing at my backside with his belt.

Arthur is a lawyer, and so there may be some difficulty
in bringing all this about. So far, in the week we've been
married, and the month of living together before, it's been
pretty tame—very sweet, very gentle, even expert, and I
come enormously and he is positively enthralled, but still:
when your ambition is to be pan-sexual, to come not just
with men and women, but at the touch of a raindrop on
your arm, at a song, over a cup of coffee, marriage is only
the second best thing—an admission of defeat, of being
pan-sexual manqué, but a way to ignite your freedom, too,
by constructing an intimacy we would naturally have if our
parents, if life, did not rob us of our first free selves and
use the offal to build its cities on. I love marriage—so far—
and I love Arthur. I trust to my instincts, and to something
smoldering about him that led him to marry a poet in the
first place. Oh, we shall see. There is more, I think, to
Arthur than meets the eye.

Sometimes I think that Hitler had a point—Adolf, not
Mark who runs the wonderful bread shop on MacDougal
Street where I used to buy my rolls, and who can be very
flamboyant ("Let *him* do it!") on the subject of changing his
name. But what I mean is: the world is so fucked up with

its murderers and banks and churches and exhausts and newspaper articles and so on that maybe it would take something, anything—even evil—that was *complete,* whole, internally and externally committed, to rescue it from what is obviously its mortal illness. I would feel a lot more sanguine about Hitler's losing the war and all if he had been defeated by something as complete as himself. But all it was was an upping of the ante—more soldiers, more generals sending them here and there, looking at maps, more patriots, more empires, and, finally, the big atomic bargaining chip, and all to stop one little man who was whole, wholly committed. If only the good guys could have come up with something new—something as *real* as he was. If, for instance, they could have locked Hitler in a room with Walt Whitman for forty-eight hours. Odds are, when the time was up, Walt would have dashed off to catch the nirvana ferry leaving Hitler to stagger out, moments later, with his asshole dripping and a beatific smile on his face to return to Vienna and paint landscapes.

All of which I mention by way of explaining how I felt about what happened to Lansky, who is a Jew, which resulted in my meeting Arthur, my beloved, my sweetikins, my guy.

Now, the way I feel about Jews is this: they know everything and they are always right. (Another reason to respect Hitler: imagine the sheer, Nietzschean will of a man who sets out to exterminate the whole truth.) It is no wonder, anyway, that they worry all the time, but this can make it very hard on those of us who, like myself, would just settle for finding out what the truth is. This is what was so frustrating for Pontius Pilate.

"What is truth?" he wanted to know.

"Don't ask," said Jesus.

Which really does remind me of many of the conversations I've had with Lansky. Lansky is a playwright, and a very funny one, too. He is tall and thin, belligerently semitic with a beaked nose and deep, fiery brown eyes, and a black goatee as sharp as his widow's peak. He is one of the gentlest, sweetest men I know and is therefore always worried that he is a wimp. As far as that goes, I myself have never made love to Lansky because I knew I would never truly love him and that made him worry that it would be too superficial, but my friend Elizabeth, who has been living with him for the past six months, says he is wonderful and attentive in bed as long as she continually reassures him that he is not having as good a time as he thinks. As you might guess, women, including myself, are frequently telling Lansky, "Don't worry, Lansky," which Lansky enjoys enormously.

Anyway, Lansky and I were sitting—38 days, thirteen hours, and seventeen minutes ago—at a table in the Black Coffee Shop, which is on MacDougal Street, a few doors down from Hitler's. Lansky's play, "The Glass Pond," had just finished a month-long engagement in a Chelsea showcase, and had actually gotten reviewed in *The New York Times*. The reviewer had compared Lansky to George Bernard Shaw, and Lansky was worried that this was so complimentary that the reviewer would feel compelled to attack him next time just to get even.

"Lansky," I remember saying, "don't worry."

"It all depends on where I open next," Lansky figured. "If I'm still off-off-Broadway, it might be okay. They usually like to really get you up there before they light into you."

Two things are on my mind while we talk, besides the conversation, in which I pretty much have one line which I have already delivered. First of all, there's some big, blond shithead giving me the eye from the table by the window. I know he is a shithead because of the way he leers as he ogles me as if to say, "What couldn't I do to *that* broad?" (answer: anything); because he is sitting alone when the place is crowded and the window table seats six; and because he is probably an NYU student and he is wearing an NYU sweatshirt.

Second of all, there is Arthur. My first impression of Arthur is that he would like very much to be part of the scene at the Black Coffee, and tell all the boys back at Gapejaw, Malevolence and Hook or wherever he works (I didn't know at that point) how he hobnobs with the student/artist set by night even though he is a straitlaced Gold

Coaster by day. The trouble is: he's hopeless, and so he is sitting there—at a two-seat table against the wall—in his polo shirt, crisp new blue jeans, white socks, and Harvards, staring shyly into his coffee cup and probably cursing the wealth of his forbears. I, while Lansky worries and Shithead stares, am repressing a powerful urge to walk across the room and stick my tongue in Arthur's ear. He is very handsome, I think, with his long, serious face and his bashful blue eyes, his strong, yes dimpled, chin, and the fine, dark-brown hair trying not to looked styled on top.

"Do you think he meant 'Major Barbara'?" Lansky is saying. "I've never liked 'Major Barbara.' It's really a terrible play: maybe he meant that one."

I am about to tell Lansky not to worry when Shithead stands up, tugs at his sweatshirt, runs his fingers through his hair—and now I am *sure* he is a shithead—and swaggers toward us. I pull a Zacharias: my tongue cleaves to the roof of my mouth, and I am mute with guilt and fear. Not for me, because before this mutt lays hand one on me I will teach him new meanings of the word "arrested." But for Lansky, who is already depressed about getting a rave in the *Times* and needs nothing less than to be humiliated in your basic antler-butting contest.

Shithead reaches our table in the center of the room, leans over me and gives me a good blast of beery breath. (This last is not true: he smelled fine, even nice, but he was the type.)

He says: "I saw you were alone and thought you could use some company."

It's a touchy situation: a line like that leaves no room for politeness, but if I tell this frog to fuck off and he retaliates, Lansky's next up with: "The lady said fuck off." Then Lansky dies which, I have a feeling, is what S.H. is after in the first place, at least subconsciously. All I can think at any rate is: "Don't get witty, Lansky," because Shithead is a big shithead and he looks like he lifts weights.

Lansky covers his eyes with his hand. "A living fart," he says. "I'm getting creamed by the critics, and a living fart has walked over to my table."

Shithead—proving my theory—is prepared for this,

though the script has skipped a couple of lines, which momentarily throws him. But, finally, he manages to turn and lour over poor, sweet Lansky.

"Listen, Big-nose," he quips, "why don't you go get yourself a prayer shawl and pray somewhere?"

"And miss this repartée?" says Lansky. "This exchange of ideas? Mercy, no." Noble Lansky.

"All right, Limpdick," says Shithead, and he steps back from the table.

I swear on the madness of Roethke that under other circumstances I would have torn this gentleman's eyes out with my own, cute little passion-red nails. But this is what I mean about Hitler: Shithead is purely, wholly, completely, one might say beautifully committed to humiliating Lansky because—I would guess—he is a Jew and knows everything and is always right *and* he is chatting and for all Shithead knows sleeping with a pretty girl, whereas Shithead knows nothing and is always wrong (witness the sweatshirt) and has about as much chance of fucking this baby as he has of learning to read in time for midterms. Now, if I scratch his eyes out—especially with me being a girl and Lansky being a boy—Lansky is duly humiliated: Shithead wins. This is also true if anyone else steps in for Lansky, and if Lansky stands up and gets creamed. In short, Shithead, through the completeness of his intention, has forced the entire universe as he knows it into conformity with himself: no matter what happens, it will happen according to his rules, unless someone comes up with something creative in a big hurry. Now, if I possessed free, body-electric, full-membership, card-carrying, amoral, radiant enlightenment, I might be swept away by the purity of Shithead's will, fall to my knees, and worship his mighty erection with my slavish tongue. Unfortunately for him, I still have my principles and if the joker comes near me, I'll slit his throat. Lansky, it seems, is on his own.

Enter the fellow in the polo shirt and Harvards who later turns out to be my Arthur, and is now walking briskly to our table, slipping between the chairs of the customers, smiling and excusing himself like the perfect gentleman I later find out he is. Arthur steps between Shithead and

Lansky, glances at the former briefly, smiles, says, "Pardon me," then hands Lansky a business card.

"My name is Arthur Clementine," he says, in a deep, dare I say melodious voice that makes my nipples tingle. "I'm with the Manhattan D.A.'s office. Just make sure you don't swing first or anything, and after he beats you up, we can pretty definitely send him to prison."

Arthur smiles and says "Excuse me," to Shithead again, bows his head to me like a cowboy tipping his hat, and strides back to his chair by the wall.

Suddenly, Lansky is beautiful; Arthur has made him beautiful. As Shithead stands dumbfounded, Lansky slips Arthur's card into his shirtpocket, leans back, folds his hands on his concave stomach, and smiles—smiles—at him.

"I just want to tell you," he says, "that I'm a psychiatrist, and I think you're a latent homosexual."

I laugh as loudly as I can.

Shithead, red-faced, sputters: "All right, Jew-boy, go ahead: hide behind the law."

At which, Lansky lets out a peal of wild, high-pitched laughter which I have no doubt will reverberate in Shithead's ears as he jerks off in his lonely dorm room that evening. After a few more curses, Shithead slinks away and I think it is then that I know I am going to marry Arthur. Because Arthur made Lansky beautiful; because Arthur wields the law against villainy, which means that he knows and accepts the world-as-it-is, which I do not, and because he made Lansky beautiful which means he understands that beauty transforms everything, even evil, into itself; and I am determined that I, and I alone, am going to be made beautiful by Arthur and give him the power of my beauty in return.

As soon as I get Lansky to stop trembling, I stand up and walk across the room to where Arthur is sitting; quickly, before I lose my confidence. He looks up: blue eyes. I extend my arm firmly.

"Allow me to shake your hand," I say, "and give you a blow job."

I am a little concerned about this approach because

Arthur, as I say, is an attorney, but he laughs outright and takes my hand and within an hour I am gleefully gulping down the chances of millions of potential Clementines to inherit the family fortune.

That's what I mean about Arthur: hidden depths.

Today is Monday, January 7th. In the newspaper, the president says he will not compromise on the military budget, the arms talks have broken down in Geneva, the governor proposes a tax cut, a rebel in El Salvador tells his story, a fundamentalist group is pocketing the money they're supposed to be sending to the starving people in Ethiopia. . . . That's all I can do. I have never been much for reading the paper, but when I said that to Arthur, he raised one lush eyebrow at me and said, "You should."

All day, I walk around repeating it to myself over and over so I will still have it when he gets home from work: "Budget, Breakdown, Tax Cut, Rebel, Fundamentalist. Budget, Breakdown, Tax Cut, Rebel, Fundamentalist. Budget, Breakdown, Tax Cut, Rebel, Fundamentalist."

When Arthur comes through the door, I run into his arms, crying, "Did you read about that big tax cut for the rebels? And how about those fundamentalists?"

But he has already hoisted me over his shoulder and is carrying me to the bedroom.

First I will tell you about my therapist, and then I will tell you about God. My therapist is named James—Doctor James—Blumenthal. About a year ago, I walked into his office, which is on Park Avenue and 86th Street, and sat on the brown easy chair, facing him.

"My name is Samantha Bradford, and I am 24," I said to him. "My usual sexual fantasy has to do with being branded."

"Please don't smoke in here," said Dr. Blumenthal—I had just put a cigarette in the corner of my mouth. "I have a problem with ventilation," he said. I put the cigarette back in the pack (that night, I had a dream about that: trying desperately to stuff the cigarette back into the pack, but it was too big) and went ahead.

"Usually," I said, "I fantasize that I am walking down the

street when a black limousine pulls up beside me, two men jump out, drag me inside and drug me. When I wake up, I'm on an island—I don't know where, but it is a place immune to international law. A handsome millionaire has bought the island—he's a dark, bearded man in his fifties but in good shape, though sometimes—"I added, "he's someone I've met or seen or a movie star, but anyway, he's assembling a seraglio and he wants me to be in it. He commands me to take my clothes off or be killed so I have to do it, and then I have to bend over this sort of bench contraption and just lie there while he takes a red-hot brand and burns his initials into my ass. Usually, if I'm masturbating or having sex, I come then—with the image of me kicking and screaming and being branded, and then, as I'm coming down from the orgasm, I see myself lying across my master's lap or at his feet, all tamed and passive while he fingers me or fucks one of his other odalisques."

Then, I stared Dr. Blumenthal directly in the eye—sort of defiantly, you might say. Dr. Blumenthal is in his late forties. He has a broad, mushy face, all pockmarked as if he had a bad case of acne when he was young. His hair is kind of grayish yellow, and very fine and falls over his forehead. Whenever he talks, just before he does, he always shifts his body in his chair as if to get more comfortable. He has a shapeless body, I guess: just a rumpled gray suit growing out of the chair.

So I look him in the eye, and he shifts a little and says: "So what seems to be the problem, Samantha?"

I start to cry. Elizabeth told me I would and I swore not to, but there it is. I think it was the way he said my name, as if I were a friend who had come to him for help.

"I tried to kill myself a while ago," I say, choking and sniffling.

Dr. Blumenthal shifts, looking concerned. "Did you succeed?"

"What?" I start to laugh at the same time I am sobbing and sobbing. Then it comes rushing out of me: "I don't want to die. I don't want to die, I'm so afraid. Can you help me?"

"It's hard to say," he says. "Depends on whether or not I

can find my branding iron."

I laugh again.

"I know it's here somewhere," he says, very serious, looking around.

Now, I am laughing more than crying, because this is not what I expected at all. When I'm finished with everything—crying, laughing, nose-blowing—I look at him, and I don't know what to say. I'm embarrassed—but it feels good to be embarrassed, it feels human, as if I have never felt human before.

Dr. Blumenthal shifts in his chair. "Tell me about the suicide attempt," he says.

The fact is, as I am very careful to explain to him because I want to be as honest about everything as I can, I don't really know whether I meant to kill myself or not or whether I just meant to pretend to kill myself. This is a big problem with me: I am never sure if I'm pretending to be something or if I am or if there's a difference.

Take my drinking, for example. For a while, I wanted everyone to think of me as this tough, cynical, hard-drinking gal who just doesn't give a damn. So I put on a good show, drinking, puking, the whole bit whenever I get a chance. By the time of my suicide attempt, I am up to almost a fifth of scotch a day, and I still think it's just an act to get my friends to respect and pity me.

On the other hand, there's sex: I have often played the hyper-experienced, seen-everything dame who has slept with more men than I care to count when really, there have only been four men in my entire life—and one was a bit of an if—excluding Arthur, and the only way I could get myself to come—even to get wet sometimes—with any of them was by thinking up elaborate fantasies like the one I described to Dr. Blumenthal.

As for my suicide attempt, what can I say? Here I still am, of course, but on the other hand if it hadn't been for Elizabeth, who knows?

I *did* have half a fifth of Clan MacGregor in me, and I *did* take an entire bottle of Demerol, which is God knows how many thousands of milligrams. But when I lay back on the bed, I was anticipating how good it was going to feel to have all my friends weeping over me when they found my body in the morning, and the exclamations of gratitude that would pour forth from them when they took me to the hospital and brought me back to life.

I do know for certain, I tell Blumenthal, that I was not expecting anyone when Elizabeth came in a few minutes later. Elizabeth Harding (of Lansky fame) is an art teacher at The School of Visual Arts. She is 33, and I would describe her as being very together. Actually, I would describe her as a goddess, my second mother—which is giving the first too much credit—my guiding light, but anyway, you get the idea. She is tall and thin and has long brown hair which is very silky and falls down her back and all these wonderful character lines on her face that make her look very kind and wise.

She comes in, using her key and calling: "Cover him up, Sam, I left my portfolio here and I need . . ."

I am trying to get out of bed but there is an anvil on my forehead. I smile at her and lie back.

Elizabeth comes over to the bedside, looks at the bottle of Clan MacGregor and the bottle of Demerol.

Then she says: "Shit."

She grabs me by the shirt collar with both hands and hauls me out of bed. She yanks me into the bathroom—I have not even got my feet under me, they are just skittering across the floor. She grabs my face in her hands, and pulls my head down over the toilet. With one hand, she squeezes my cheeks until my mouth opens, with the other, she sticks her fingers down my throat while I claw at her arms trying to stop her.

I vomit—tons of undigested capsules and amber scotch—I vomit forever, all over the toilet, over Elizabeth, over myself. Finally, I am on my knees, retching, and there is nothing left.

Then Elizabeth grabs me by the hair and says, "Get up," and pulls me to my feet. I see her face is very red and her cobalt eyes are burning. I do not think I have ever seen her this angry. She slaps me in the face so hard my head snaps back, my hair flying. I put up my hands but she knocks them down and slaps me again. I am crying and groaning—I feel awful—and Elizabeth is screaming, "How dare you?" over and over again in a voice that does not even sound like hers. She cuffs me a good one on the side of the head, and then she throws me against the wall and screams, "I'm sick of you, Sam. Go to hell. Do you understand? Just go to hell." She does not seem to know what she's saying.

When she is through yelling, she turns and walks right out the door, slamming it behind her. I hear her footsteps going down the stairs, and I slide down the bathroom wall to the floor, sobbing because I am all alone in the world and no one loves me.

Finally, I grab hold of the sink and pull myself to my feet, still sniffling. I stagger into the other room, and stand there for a minute not knowing what to do next—almost as if there's a script for this but I've forgotten my lines.

Then there are footsteps on the stairs again. Elizabeth comes back through the door, and just stands in front of me, looking at me. She is crying, too, and trembling—with rage, I think. I hang my head. I am ashamed though I don't know why she's so mad at me. I am also afraid she will hit me again.

She hits me again, so hard this time I just topple right over like a young dogwood I once saw blown down in a hurricane back home. I fall over on the bed and lie there sobbing. Elizabeth storms into the kitchenette and begins to make coffee.

It is Elizabeth who gives me Dr. Blumenthal's name, which she got from her therapist. I tell her I cannot afford therapy, but Elizabeth says Dr. Blumenthal will lower his rates to accommodate me because he is interested in the creative mind. I tell her that therapy will tamper with my muse, but she forces me to admit that death might do the same thing. I tell her that therapy will not work unless I *want* to go, but she says that's too bad and this therapy will have to work because *she* wants me to go. I do not protest very much after that because I feel I have made a terrible mess of things, but it does take me more than a month to make an appointment with Dr. Blumenthal.

When I leave Dr. Blumenthal's office after that first visit,

I feel as I have never felt before in my life. It is March, and the sky is blue and the air cool, and Park Avenue is a great row of brilliantly green traffic lights running down to the Helmsley Building and the Pan Am Building rising behind that and there are clouds sailing over them that seem to me like the ships of some ghostly nation migrating to a new country, a new life that will set its people's history on a fruitful and promising course. Suddenly, I realize that I have never written a good poem, never had a fulfilling orgasm, never truly tasted the sweetness of chocolate ice cream, or seen the clouds or the buildings or the trees, or known peace—and that all this unhappiness has been *unnecessary*—completely unnecessary when there all along sat Dr. Blumenthal waiting to take it off my shoulders.

I am not a fool, I know that this elation will not last, that there is all manner of work to be done, of terrors to be faced, of dragons to be slain before I ever see this golden country again. But now that I have seen it, I will keep it in my mind and remember it so I will know what I am fighting for, where I am traveling.

I leave Park Avenue behind, and head for Third where there is a Baskin Robbins. I must have some chocolate ice cream—quick, before it melts.

Which brings me to God and penises. After three months or so of seeing Dr. Blumenthal twice a week, I find I am thinking about penises constantly. Not thinking about them exactly, more like singing about them, dreaming about them, inhabiting the idea of them. To be honest, this has never happened to me before, even when I was a teen-ager. In fact, I feel like a teen-ager as I walk the streets of Manhattan, secretly staring at businessmen's zippers, blushing, smiling. Cocks. Before, I always thought of them—I did not realize it before but—with some distaste, as if they were an exposed piece of intestine or a dangling blood vessel. Now, they appear to me like lovely, spreading oak trees, or tender stalks shooting out of the earth, only I am not thinking of trees or stalks—I am thinking about pricks. Sleek, silky, hard, pink, salty, motile, probing—certain words begin to make me crazy. Pink. Hard. Mush-

room. The word spurt mentioned casually in conversation
makes me lick my lips and go all drowsy. "Hey, Sam, let's
spurt over to the hardware store for some salty, pink
mushrooms. Sam? Sam?" I begin to write odes. I have
never had much use for the ode before.

I am ceaselessly tingling, frustrated—because I am also,
suddenly, very shy—but also awake to the pleasure of
anticipation. Forever will I love and he be fair. I begin
wearing skirts for easy access, fantasize—prowling the
streets, studying the crotches—of leaving my panties at
home, of bending over, lying back, opening my mouth
anywhere and everywhere for the feel of the sudden
thrust, thrust, the easy slide of a pink, hard, salty, mushrooming prick. What a world of pleasure it is.

Anyway, about this time, I volunteer for the hotline. I do
this on an impulse after seeing a sign in the YMCA where
Lansky's latest is being performed, but it is pretty clear to
me: I am beginning to identify with Dr. Blumenthal or, at
least, need to feel myself in a position of power over others
as he is over me. Whatever.

The hotline—Lifeline, it is called—is a place for people
to call when they are suicidal or depressed. In a six-week
training course, we are taught to listen sympathetically, not
to give advice, try to draw out the painful issues—stuff I
feel I have already picked up from watching Jimbo do his
thing.

I am set to work in a little cubicle in the bottom of St.
Sebastian's on West 48th Street near Tenth Avenue. My
shift is Thursday from two to six and my partner is a dried
out stick of a woman named Patricia who speaks through
her nose. Most of the people who call are chronic—depressed, complainers. I listen and try to be friendly,
though I find myself analyzing them, which we are not
supposed to do. The truth is, I find it very relaxing: the
only four hours in the week when I am not thinking about
my own problems. I also hope it will give me some material
for poetry.

It is, I think, sometime in July when I get a call from a
man with a deep, dull voice and a heavy Queens accent. I
am still thinking about penises, though not as much as

before, but that is what I am thinking about when he calls
and says:
"Who's this?"
"This is Samantha," I say earnestly. "What's your name?"
"This is God," he says. "Call me God."
I should say at this point that I have always considered
myself a very spiritual person, although just lately I have
begun to notice that the larger part of my spirituality
consists in the fear that God will give me cancer if I am
bad. Every time I get a stomach ache, which is frequently, I
am convinced that it is a tumor, and it is then you will find
me kneeling under the altarpiece of St. Thomas' Cathedral, bargaining away my freedom of thought for a few
more years of cohabitation with my uterus. I am, in short,
very superstitious—knock wood—and when this caller tells
me he is God I find myself entertaining the proposition
that he really is. He doesn't sound much like Him, on the
one hand; on the other hand, the idea that the source of
creation is located somewhere around Flushing really does
explain a lot.
"How can I help you?" I say.
"I'm gonna kill myself," says God.
"Uh huh." He says nothing. I try wit: "Some people say
that God is already dead."
Monotone, I get: "No, but I will be if this keeps up."
"What seems to be the problem?"
"Oh, you know, it's like first you're eternal, it's great,
you're always creative, but you're always destructive, too.
Everything keeps changing. I want something solid, some
joy, laws. So right away I'm making laws, I'm also making
time, I'm getting imprisoned in the senses. It sucks."
To be frank, I am already bored with this: God calling
up a suicide hotline is not so much a philosophical irony as
it is a one-liner. As he speaks, I am casting about for ways
to elicit some humanity from this poor bastard, something
interesting. Suddenly, it comes to me. Of all the Lifeline
volunteers, this guy has called the one person who might
be able to help him. This has never happened before and I
am very excited by the sense of power it gives me.
I throw out a feeler. "I pity you," I say.

"That's just it!" he says excitedly. "I pity myself, and pity divides the soul."

I've got him: he's been reading Blake! Well, no wonder he's gone crazy. "You feel another part of you coming out," I say.

Sullenly; caught: "Yeah."

"What you might call a feminine part."

A pause. "What did you say your name was?"

I grin. "Samantha. Sam. What did you say your name was?"

I hear him sigh. "Listen—could you just call me God for now?"

"Sure."

"I gotta go, okay?" Another pause; longer. "Are you there all the time?"

"Thursdays, two to six," I say.

"I'll call back, okay?"

"Okay, God," I say, and he hangs up.

I feel wonderful—I have helped someone—I have connected—someone needs me. This in itself, I tell myself grandly, is a more interesting aspect of God: the idea of two human beings connecting, interlocking, becoming a whole. It is an act of love, I keep repeating to myself: an act of love.

I am still thinking about this when I walk into Dr. B's the next morning: an act of love. I tell him about God which I figure is all right because, even though Lifeline is totally confidential, so is therapy, though I can't help thinking I am becoming part of a long chain of dark secrets that will end with everybody knowing everything.

"He was lucky you knew your Blake," says D.B.

"Yes—well: I'm a poet," I say superciliously—because Doctor B is *not* a poet, you understand.

His gray suit shifts in his chair. "I've never really understood Blake," he says—sheepishly, as if he is confessing something.

This just hangs there in the air for a few moments while I am feeling something inside me like one of those slow motion pictures of the underwater atomic bomb tests—something rising from the depths, mushrooming, spurting into the air. My lips begin to tremble and my eyes get moist. I have not cried since that first visit four months ago, and I do not want to now; it is one of my few bastions of pride still left standing with this man.

"There's something I haven't told you," I say, and I hate the little girl tremor in my voice.

"Oh?"

"Something about my fantasy—the one I told you about, about being branded. I haven't had it in a long time. Well, not as much. I used to always have it, I hardly ever do anymore. But back when I had it, back then—it wasn't always a man with the branding iron. It used to be." Fuck it: I'm crying. "When I started first having the fantasy it was. But then more and more, I started thinking about a woman. . . ."

I think this is disgusting enough for one session, but Blumenthal says: "Anyone in particular?"

I shake my head. "No," I say. Then I say, "Yes. Sometimes. Elizabeth."

"And when you tried to kill yourself?"

"I knew the portfolio was there. I knew she'd left it there."

"You wanted her to find you."

"I wanted her to show—" Why is it so hard to say? "I wanted her to show that she loved me."

"By getting angry at you."

"What?" I am sobbing.

Blumenthal shifts. "You wanted her to show that she loved you by getting angry at you."

I frown—I can only describe it as petulantly—at him, jutting out an accusing chin. "Are we talking about my mother?"

"Are we?" he asks, which is exactly why people hate psychiatrists.

I slump. "I guess we are," I say.

Which really does explain a lot, also, about my feelings toward Lansky, when you come to think about it, since he is living with Elizabeth now, which sort of puts him into my father's position—wimpy, but all-knowing—and then Shithead comes along, just this ignorant, ravenous, repre-

sentative of sheer Power, and there am I, caught between
them, tongue-tied, frozen—and then, suddenly, a third
choice, another way of loving: Arthur, descending with
the law like Apollo before Orestes, so that I need be
neither a scarred victim nor a mutant oppressor, but something else entirely: an orchid, a giant orchid blossoming
out of the pines.

Oh, I am *so* glad to have found Arthur!

# Two

For money, I used to work as a reader—a story analyst, it
is called—for a movie studio. What I did was read books
and screenplays and then write synopses of them and say
whether or not they would make a good film. This is a
wonderful job for a poet, as you can make your own hours
and take on as much or as little work as you need. Sometimes, though, I used to feel as if all the stories of the world
were being laid at my feet—all the fantasies, the rage.
Especially after I began seeing Dr. Blumenthal, I began to
feel that every novel was simply an expression of someone's twisted personality. I would read a thriller, for example, about some knife-wielding maniac butchering up
women and I would know that that was something going
on in the author's mind—although it must have been going
on in the audience's minds, too, or no one would buy it.
Every now and again, I would read a good book that would
disprove my theory: that is, it was still about the author,
but it was about everybody, too, and thinking about the
author was just a way of avoiding thinking about yourself.
Anyway, I can see why people like to make movies instead
of writing books: you can always blame a movie on someone else.

Reading was not exactly up there with, say, being a cop
for excitement. In fact, I have never seen people work less
than in the movie business. Where I worked there was a
Story Editor, a whiny princess named Dorothy, and her
assistant (read: secretary), a nice-enough woman named
Judy, and between the two of them I don't know how—or

if—anything ever got done. Sometimes, I would come into the office to pick up my assignment and it would be like walking into a Beckett play:

On a bare stage: two desks, a movie poster hanging on the wall. At each desk, a woman sits. One is *Barrow,* the other *Dolmen.*

Barrow: I'm so bored.
Dolmen: Should we do something?
Barrow: Yes, let's.
Dolmen: What should we do?
*A pause.*
Barrow: We could go home.
Dolmen: Yes, that's an idea. Oh wait:
 is it five yet?
Barrow: Where's the clock? I can't find the clock!
Dolmen: There's no God!
Barrow: I'm so bored.

In the year and a half I was with the company, not one story I recommended was ever bought by the bosses in California. Through me, these stories flowed, were transformed into synopses, and vanished into an abyss wherein echoed words like, "Too downbeat. Not cinematic. Too internal." Odd, because I had taken the job because the real world demands you make money, even if you are a poet, and yet nothing I did ever had the slightest effect on a single other human being.

All of which I suppose is by way of getting round to the subject of money, which is I think the world's excrement and is, as I say, always a problem for a poet, Daughter of Eros that she is.

I quit my job when I married Arthur. Arthur is one of the Philadelphia Clementines so even though he works for the city, he is well-to-do. I always joke that the Clementines made their fortune in gold mines, but the fact is the money is so old no one can remember where it came from and it is just attributed to some form of vague plunder which occurred back in the days when plunder was something simply everyone was doing. Now, I am Samantha Clementine, living off their riches, and about fifteen dollars a month for my poems. From plunder to poetry, that is the way of the world.

Today, February 22nd, there is a big headline on the front page of the *Times,* which either means something very important has happened, or they didn't have enough stories to fill up the page and so had to stretch one. The headline reads: "Soviets Accuse U.S. of Mining Nicaraguan Ports." And under that: "Sec. of State Flies to Geneva." At first, I think the Sec. of State is running away, dumping the whole mess in the lap of the President, who has already absconded to Camp David for another vacation. Wouldn't it be funny if the whole thing fell to the White House janitor: "I got ten thousand square feet of rug to vacuum. When am I mining harbors, in my sleep?" Anyway, the Sec. is really going to meet with the Soviet Ambassador, so it is all under control and I draw the veil on their tender reunion in order to move on to this far more interesting piece: "Scientists Say Ten Percent Of The Universe Is Missing." Now, *this* could be serious, although it'll probably turn up when they clean. Without this ten percent, apparently, the universe will just keep expanding and expanding until everything turns to ashes and dies. This is too much for these scientists to bear and they are desperately inventing theories as to where this ten percent could be. With the added weight, the universe will expand to a certain point, and then come together again into a sort of primordial spaulding which will explode and start the whole process over again. This the scientists can live with, though I personally recommend short-term investments. All this just goes to prove that science is no more than the search for reassurance from the perceived world that our *a priori* intimations are valid. Once we understand that perceptions and intimations are one, the scientists can go home and, even as things stand, it seems to me, the Secretary of State should relax and try to get in a little skating.

Don't get me wrong: it's not that I mind being a housewife. We only have a two-bedroom apartment to begin with, and a maid comes in once a week to clean. (Arthur calls her "a woman," as if that were a job description: she is a maid, which, now I think of it, means the same thing.) In fact, it is this that worries me: there is not really that much for me to do. I write poetry every morning after Arthur goes to work, but I am done by about one, and then no matter how much I linger over the *Times* and my carrot salad, by two-thirty I am beginning to feel like a scientist contemplating a universe with ten percent missing. I mean, I am beginning to feel as if maybe I am not a very important person.

Last night, Arthur comes home, and we have a conversation that brings this to light. I have seen him getting out of the cab (we live on Fifth Avenue and 81st, doncha know) and so when he comes through the door, I am draped naked over an armchair that has been in the family for centuries, with my legs spread and my open cunt just at the right level for him to make a beeline into ecstasy.

Instead, he comes over, kisses me lightly on the pudenda, and says, "Hi, honey, I'm home. Boy, you need a shave."

At first, I think he is proposing something really interesting, but when this is followed by silence, I lift my head and see him standing over me, still dressed, his handsome face drawn and weary.

"Would you like to make a drink first how about?" he says with a little apologetic smile.

Now he is sitting on the sofa, which has been in the Clementine family for centuries, sipping a martini while I, who have been in the Clementine family for seven weeks, lie naked with my head in his lap, watching my breasts rise and fall and reflecting without rancor on the fact that it has been three full weeks now since I have consumed an alcoholic beverage of any kind.

"What did you do today?" says Arthur, stroking the hair on my forehead.

"I wrote a poem about that pigeon I saw in front of the museum I told you about? The one who had lost both his feet and he could fly but he couldn't walk. I'll bet he had a hard time landing, too, but that's not in the poem. What did you do?"

He heaves a heavy sigh. "Oh, we processed a couple of 15-year-olds who tossed an infant off a roof."

"Oh God. Why?"

"There was nothing on TV, they said," says Arthur. "The victim was one of the kids' younger brothers."

Arthur is a little down about this, I can tell, and so after he finishes his drink, I minister to him tenderly, undressing him, sucking him, and finally sliding myself onto him until he rears up and shoots what must have been a very wicked day into my womb.

But behind the Florence Nightingale of sex there lurks a murky phantom of discontent. Because all I can think as I slide up and down that sleek, slim, long, white pole that I call friend is: Why do I always have to make the drinks? I don't even drink anymore. Why don't you make your own drinks? You think you're more important than I am because you process 15-year-old babykillers? Writing poetry about pigeons is no holiday, you know. Oily, dirty little birds.

Perturbation reigns. This is the first time I have ever gotten pissed at Arthur.

My mother did nothing. I don't want to give the impression that I am one of these people who blames her mother for everything that's wrong with me. Personality is a great mystery after all and what affects one person one way is not necessarily oh fuck it she was a bitch. Cold, beautiful, statuesque: I swear to God I never saw her lips part. She ground my father into the earth so quietly, so wittily, so subtly that he didn't know his balls were gone until she swallowed them—until she shit them, left them floating on the surface of the toilet water just so there'd be no mistake. I am done forgiving her. I will never be done loving her, but I am done forgiving her forever.

She sat . . . We lived in Greenwich, Connecticut. My father was a stock consultant and we were quite well-to-do, thank you very much, though not to say loaded. She sat, my mother did, in that colonial mansion he built for her, wrested for her from the rats scrambling all over Wall Street, she sat and she did nothing. She must have done something. She must have eaten and I can't remember her being fed by any of the countless Consuelas, or Rosas or Floras who knelt to wash her kitchen floor for her, but when I think of her I remember her sitting, erect, motionless, enthroned like a statue of Hatshepsut on a rosewood chair. I remember her profile, the lips set, her hands moving out to play Patience, to point out some chore for Consuela or Rosa or Flora, to hit me.

Actually, she only hit me once. I was three and had torn a page in a book—a copy of the *Inferno*, now I think of it, with the illustrations by Blake. I remember being fascinated with those engravings, those nude forms swirling in circles through the air as if torment were motion, and then the page tore and her hand shot out as if to move a red seven to a black eight and she backhanded me without a word and took the book away and lay it on the table before her, next to the cards. Later, I remember going upstairs to play with my brother's fire truck, running a little figure up the ladder, rising with him until I slammed my head on the edge of the end table where the fire was supposed to be. I started to cry, silently, and then I ran the figure up the ladder again and slammed my head again; then I just lifted my head and slammed it. Christ.

Later on—I mean, years later, when I was fifteen, and I came home late from school, and she knew, I don't know how she knew, that I had done it, that Michael and I had gone to bed together though I don't think she could have known how miserably, how painfully, how joylessly, stupidly, bloodily we had accomplished our mission with Michael following his erection as if it were a rocket tied to his groin, dragging him along with hands over his eyes and me believing, oh, I don't know, that I had a soul, maybe, that the full, rounded breasts I had not asked for, the gaping, oozing scar between my legs, the curve of my legs, all of it, was not me somehow, when it was, it was all along, all of me, and whatever soul I had was not disconnected from it, but part of it, composed of it, so that when

Michael, of the denims, the toughness, the sad, ridiculous
burden of teen-aged masculinity broke the membrane finally after his knees were torn to pieces by the buttons of
his mattress, when he jammed into me, was jamming into
*me*, lying on top of *me* like a fallen building, pumping and
gasping, "I'm sorry, I'm sorry," while I tried to fight him
off because I thought he was killing *me* and all my mother
knew was that we had "done it" whatever that meant to her,
whatever part of "it" meant to her that she was weakened
somehow, that I had put one over on her, become part of
the Big Cheat which surrounded her rosewood chair like
an aura, which could only be avoided, placated, by absolute
stillness, motionlessness, and here her own daughter . . .
She said to me: "When you go to sleep tonight, I am going
to come into your room with a pair of scissors and cut off
all your hair." Black jack on red queen. Hi, Mom, I'm
home. What's for dinner?

She didn't do it, though I didn't sleep for a couple of
nights. I suppose she was half mad by then between meno-
pause and the smell of perfume that my father could never
quite get off his clothing, poor man. Her own father had
deserted her mother for another woman. Her mother had
had to go to jail once—just for a night before my great-
uncle bailed her out—because she refused to pay off her
husband's debts with money she considered hers. Maybe I
should forgive her in the name of history, for the way
history has of appearing to us like a series of photographs
in a row or a movie but being really one frame, one picture
that has been exposed and exposed and exposed again by a
shutter that never closes.

But verily, verily, I say unto you: My hair is auburn and
cascades over my shoulders like a river of honeyed wine.
There is no other color on earth like the color of my hair.

God is not without something to say on this subject,
though what the subject is I'm not too sure. The second
time he called me was about two weeks after the first so it
was still summer. I picked up the phone with my usual
soft, deep, earnest, caring, "Lifeline," and he says: "Get
fucked."

"If you are going to be abusive, I am going to have to hang up," I say, which is what I've been taught to say in training.

"This is God," he says sheepishly, by way of explanation, and I figure, oh well, if it's the Almighty, I'll take a *little* abuse. "I just don't want you to be too serene about this, and superior."

"Got it," I say. "I'm agitated and groveling, go on."

"No, I mean: you are a woman. You're supposed to *like* getting fucked, but it's an insult. You shoot someone the bird, it's an insult, but you're supposed to *like* getting the bird. If you act tough, someone says, 'You've got balls.' If you act tender, no one ever says, 'Hey, you got real breasts, lady. You're what I call a cunt.' "

I laugh.

"I'm serious," he says.

I stop laughing.

"No one ever compliments you by saying you're a cunt because it's an insult to be a cunt. It means you've got no balls." He says this last so quietly, so sadly, that my heart really does go out to God, and I wish I could reach out and stroke his hair.

"Well," I say, "it's an insult to be a prick, too."

"You shouldn't curse," says God. "You're a lady."

He's right: I'd forgotten for a moment that I'm dealing with a psychotic.

"Anyway, that's why I've gotta kill myself," he says. "To create Death again, to bring Death back into the world."

I'm not entirely sure I get the connection but, on reflection, I am entirely sure I don't know what he's talking about, so I try to move us back to what I think is the subject.

"What you're saying is that out of your great power, your almightiness, something else is emerging. Something, in fact, you had to become almighty to suppress: something tender, that makes you afraid you're losing your ba— manhood." Before I catch myself, I nearly shift in my chair.

"And don't tell me about the feminists!" God shouts.

"Oh no. As far as I'm concerned you should never have created those feminists," I say. "And gnats."

"They've just accepted the whole thing, just like they always did only now they figure if it's better to be a man, they will be—or ca-ca-ca-castrate the men, one or the other. I mean, who *says* it's better to be a businessman than a mother?"

"Not me."

"Who says it's better to wear a suit than a dress?"

"Not me."

"What do businessmen do that's so important, anyway?"

"Damned if I know."

"So now don't you see why I have to create Death?"

"Oh, I don't know," I say without thinking. "Why don't you just create Love instead?"

And he begins screaming: "Love *is* Death, that's what I'm saying! Don't you understand anything, you stupid cunt?"

I have no answer. I wait in silence. Then, I hear something, a stuttering, a squeaking on the other end. God is crying.

"I'm so unhappy," he says. "I'm so unhappy."

"I know," I say into the phone. "But it's all right, now. I'm here. I'm here."

After a while, the sound begins to subside. "I think I have to go," he says.

"Will you call back if you need to?"

"Yes." I wait. He is still there. He sniffles. "You know," he says. "You really are a cunt."

I smile. "Thank you," I say.

And he's gone.

There's something to be said, I guess, for God's theory, except I have a theory about theories, which is: theories are like a horse that can't swim: it will carry you to the River of Enlightenment, but it can't get you across. That takes experience: satori: a kick in the eye. Which is why we have art. And meditation. And psychotherapy. We already know how to spell the word "fist," what we are looking for is a good punch in the mouth.

Just lately, to be honest, I have been regaling Dr. Blumenthal with nothing but theories: ideas, intellectualizations, thoughts, ponderings, little things I've noticed in my perambulations. Anything but life. This gives me a sense of power. I have a fantasy that slowly, almost without his knowing it, my subconscious is taking him over, growing up inside him like some sort of inflatable Blumenthal that will eventually break through his skin and replace the Blumenthal of the moment. Already, I notice, he is making little Clementinian slips: small things: he forgot to send me a bill one month, and once, when I told him a particularly terrible nightmare I had about being trapped in a roomful of mice, he said: "And so this really scared me—you."

This, of course, is only to be expected. I am a poet, after all: my subconscious is everybody's problem.

This morning, the day after I got annoyed at Arthur, I am explaining to Blumenthal my theory about theories, called to the surface by my memory of God, called up in turn by my annoyance with Arthur, neither of which I have bothered to mention, they being secondary to my T of T's.

"This," I explain, "is why I am trying to create a poetry of pure description, of objects, because these are the things that make up life and we never *see* them, not really. I have been living in Arthur's apartment going on three months now, and how often does it come to life for me, does it become real? How often do I really *see* the scroll of the mahogany legs of the sofa, the way the shag looks far away through the glass coffee table, even the Degas ballerina or the handmade colonial quilt on the bed. I mean, I make it every morning, but . . . "

"He has a Degas?" says Blumenthal, proving my point because that's exactly what *I* said when I first saw it.

"Yes," I say, "it's a . . . "

"A genuine Degas? A real one?"

"Well, it's just a small one. His mother gave it to him when he graduated law school."

"Wow," says Blumenthal. "A real Degas, huh?"

Now, I am getting annoyed, but I manage to say with perfect calm: "Are you trying to tell me something?" "Yes," says Blumenthal. He shifts in his chair. "I wish I had a Degas." "Well, then you make his lousy drinks." At which point, the session comes to an end.

Two weeks after I moved in with Arthur, I was invited to a party given by Jake Langley. Jake is a somewhat famous poet which, basically, means that his obscurity has limits, that it does not, in effect, threaten to collapse upon itself from its own density like a dead star. Jake lives in Westchester where he teaches, so Lansky, Elizabeth, Arthur and I all drove up in Arthur's car.

It was a dark and stormy night. Ice was streaking out of the black sky like falling daggers, and twice Elizabeth had to wrestle Lansky to the floor to keep him from offering Arthur money to get him to pull over. The last stretch was the worst because Jake lives in a cottage at the end of a dirt road, basically in the middle of the woods. When the lights of the cottage appeared to us through the gloom, Lansky made a sound like a cross between a church choir singing "Gloria in excelsis" and a mongrel dog baying at the moon.

No one but us, of course, had shown up: us, Jake, his current lover Humphrey, a painter named Stephanie, who was over from England and staying with Jake, and a woman named Isabella Gardner.

Humphrey made us all drinks and we sat in the living room with ice streaking the big windowpanes on every wall, and the trees bending and the wind blowing and it was very cozy even with Lansky continually wondering aloud about how we were going to get home. About an hour or so into the conversation, however, it begins to become very clear to me that Isabella Gardner is insane. She is a short, somewhat dumpy woman, but with a fresh, open, corn-fed face and wide blue eyes. Most of the time, she sits smiling beatifically, turning her intense gaze from speaker to speaker. But when Arthur tells a story about a rock concert he went to where tear gas from the riot outside (Arthur, by the way, is 33) seeped in and forced the audience to come pouring out, thereby routing the police, Isabella nods and smiles as if she knows all and says: "Oh yes, that happened to me once, too. My father was giving a concert, but then his intestines poured out on the stage and so I was arrested. Then the witches came."

There is a moment of embarrassed silence and then Arthur says: "Well—that sure tops my story." Everybody laughs—Isabella, too—and the conversation goes on and a minute later I, for one, cannot be sure whether I actually heard Isabella correctly or not.

But after a few minutes, Jake brings out the first copy of his new book, *Castigating Croesus,* for us to admire. It really is admirable, with woodcuts by Stephanie depicting, in a vague, suggestive way, the shadows of the Greek gods hovering over modern cityscapes. We pass the book around, oohing and ahing because this is what the party was for and now the bad weather has robbed Jake of the warmth, appreciation and stifled envy of his friends.

When Isabella gets the book, she lays it on her lap and begins turning the pages, carefully smoothing them down with her open hand. Conversation progresses. Then Isabella says: "Ooh, there's the autopsy."

Jake leans over to see with a worried look on his face.

"They used to let me do it until I began to eat the brains," quips Isabella. "I never made him suffer, though. I always sewed him up again before my mother got home." She smiles rather beautifully at Stephanie, pinning her to the sofa in terror. "I didn't know you were there," she says.

Lansky is now whispering feverishly to Elizabeth who is poking him in the ribs with her elbow. Arthur casts me a look and Jake is still trying to figure out how a picture of an autopsy got into his book. Only Humphrey is smiling, perfectly relaxed, and I begin to suspect that Isabella's invitation is not without its motive vis à vis interpersonal relationships.

Suddenly, Humphrey claps his hands together, and says, "Oh, I know, let's play 'Murder'!"

"Murder," for those who do not know, is a game in which each person gets dealt a playing card and the one who gets the Ace of Spades or whatever is the murderer. The lights are turned off and everyone runs around in the dark until the murderer taps him on the shoulder. Then he lies down dead until he is discovered, at which point the discoverer lets out a harrowing scream, the lights go on, and everyone tries to guess who did it. This is why Lansky's eyes have turned the size of saucers and he is braving Elizabeth's elbow in order to get in a few more frantic whispers.

In truth, I am more than a little scared myself. I know exactly what is going to happen. The lights go off—wander, wander, wander—a shriek—lights on—to reveal someone's decapitated body—mine, more than likely—with Isabella kneeling over it, smiling beatifically, if a tad bloodily, while she devours the victim's brain.

Still in all, even Lansky isn't coward enough to protest aloud. The cards are duly dealt—I get an eight of hearts—and Humphrey gleefully kills the light.

My plan is simple. Keep track of Arthur and, when the lights go out, throw myself, trembling, into his arms and wait for the ordeal to end. In the event, however, Humphrey hits the switch and we are plunged into a forest darkness deeper than I have ever known. Arthur is gone. I am lost, wandering about with my hands out in front of me, bumping my shins against all manner of unseen terrors.

I wander this way for three weeks—or possibly five minutes, I cannot tell—with shadows flitting on every side of me, making me jump, and an occasional maniacal giggle by way of reassurance. I wander by the kitchen and hear a drawer open, cutlery rattle: Isabella is getting herself a butcher knife, no doubt, so I betake the vessel of the muse to distant territories, wandering into a room with which I am unfamiliar.

There, she grabs me. Someone grabs me, and at first it doesn't matter who because whether he is going to kill me or not is irrelevant: my heart has stopped. Then, to my unutterable relief, I see the gleaming eyes and horror-stricken face of Lansky.

"You're dead, Sam," he whispers. "Wish I was."

I know what he means. I am so glad to be dead I want to kiss him. Now I can sit down against a wall, safe from harm, and wait until I or some other fortunate is discovered and the lights come on again.

I sit down against the wall, facing the room's only door, which I see as a rectangle of the dimmest gray in the blackness. I wait. Minutes go by—slowly, but a lot more like minutes than when I was wandering around with that knife-wielding father-killer on the loose. No one can come through the door without my seeing them. I wait and wait.

Then, a silhouette on the dim rectangle. It pauses, enters. It is Arthur!

"Arthur! Arthur!" I hiss. "Over here!"

He comes over, pausing on the way to bark his shin and curse. Then he is standing above me.

"Sam?"

"Arthur! Scream," I say. "Discover me, so they'll turn the bloody lights back on."

"What's the matter, Sam?" he says. "Scared?" He kneels down in front of me.

"Yes, I'm scared! Why would I want you to scream if I wasn't scared, you idiot?" say I.

I feel Arthur's hands on my jeans, unzipping my fly, passing inside, down over my pubic hair to my vagina, which begins to gush at once in my high-pitched state of jumbled terror, relief, frustration and excitement.

"So you want me to scream," says Arthur, several of his fingers, maybe his whole hand, swimming into this hot fountain between my legs.

"Yes!" I hiss, but I am giggling now. Panting and giggling.

"What will you give me?" says Arthur.

"Anything, anything."

"Will you marry me, Sam?"

"What?" I have an orgasm: a small one, but elegant and I am amused by its presumption.

"I love you, Samantha," says Arthur. "Will you marry me?"

"Oh. Oh, Arthur." I am gushing, it seems, from both ends. "Oh yes. Yes."

His hand slips out of my cunt and he lets out a shriek so loud, so high-pitched that I am sure it will shatter one of the two glass candle holders that Jake is so proud of.

There is the sound of footsteps approaching. Lights go on around the house. Quickly, I zip up my jeans. Lansky—in an effort, no doubt, to avoid the appearance of guilt—is the first into the room. He snaps on the light. The glare hurts my eyes and I turn to one side.

And I am face to face with the beatific smile of Isabella, who has been sitting not six inches away from me all this time.

My reaction to this little revelation, I suspect, takes care of the other candle holder.

It just came to me with a great shock that Arthur's name is Arthur. Or not exactly a great shock, so much as a sort of reverberating *pip!* but all the same what makes it so shocking, or so pipping, is that that is *King* Arthur's name, too, the pip here deriving from the fact that I am, or was, something of a King Arthur fanatic.

The craze has passed now but there was a time—it's so odd that this did not occur to me before—when Arthur, King not my, inhabited all my days. It began about five years ago, while I was still in school, when Richard Burton brought the revival of the Lerner and Lowe musical "Camelot" to Lincoln Center. To be exact, it began when Burton, who was much shorter than I had imagined and seemed to me to have something of an oversized head, peered lugubriously off-stage and sang:

"Don't let it be forgot,
That once there was a spot,
For one brief shining moment,
That was known
As
Camelot."

The point being that the great civilization of the Round Table had fallen because Lancelot and Queen Guinevere had been at it and, anyway, I wept, I don't mind confess-

ing. I went home and began reading. I read T. H. White's
*Once And Future King,* and then Tennyson's "Idylls," then
Malory's *Morte,* then Chrétien De Troyes' romances and
then Geoffrey De Tours' *History*—down, down, down into
the funnel of time, hoping, I think, to find that springboard of truth on whch I could vault back to the pageantry
and romance of Richard Burton singing, hauling credulity
with me by the collar. I have always been something of an
exacting romantic. Instead, what I got was "Sir Gawain
And The Green Knight." I was far from where I'd started
by then, because what I really loved was Arthur the wise,
Arthur the grave, Arthur the tragic (Burton, in short) and
this was just knight stuff, but I hadn't got past the first
line—which was something like "Since the siege of Troy
. . . " when up turned my springboard where I had least
expected it. It was this: civilization falls when Woman,
lovely Woman, chooses youth and virility over wisdom and
age. God-Satan, Laius-Oedipus, Menelaus-Paris, Arthur-
Lancelot, Lansky-Shithead, the wise father or the virile
son: that was the choice that was put before us from Eden
on, and all we ladies had to do was get just a dose of the
hots for the young stuff and you could say your bye-byes
to sweet paradyes. This, I confess, was way too deep for
me because it was not just father-son, but, by corollary,
mind-body, brow-groin, soul-flesh that was at issue here;
and as a representative of those who had to point the
finger like some matron in front of a shelf at the super-
market and say, "Oh, I'll take this one," I felt as if I had just
discovered that all detergents cause cancer and the only
really good way to get your clothes clean is to rub them in
grass and chant.

Because it struck me in a flash (i.e., developed as a
thought over the period of the next few days) that it was all
an illusion. A terrible mistake. When men say: "Men are
rational, women passionate," what they really mean is, "I
am rational until I see a dame and then I can't think
straight," just as when a woman says, "Men are domineering and insensitive," she means, "I am in charge until a
man comes by and then I have an urge to submit, and turn
to him for validation of myself." Arthur, Lancelot *and*

Guinevere were all parts of the body politic—a psycho-machy—which led me to believe that we cannot see any-thing in our opposite but ourselves. We can't. We Kant. We cant. And so if rationality looking at passion is really pas-sion looking at rationality and vice versa, if the Father, the Son, and the Holy Ghost, absence, cunt, woman are, as they say, truly one, why do I begin to feel that marrying Arthur, that marrying Arthur was . . . what? A betrayal? A mistake? A loss?

Blumenthal is a geek and he can just shut up, too. We are not talking about my father. (Aren't we?) Not yet we're not, kiddo. I have theories you haven't even dreamed of yet. Wait'll you get a load of my resolution of the Plato-Aristotle dilemma. And, anyway, there was a moment, there was a day, a night, when we came home from Jake's when we had sent Elizabeth up the stairs with Lansky, a dishrag of exhausted terror, in her arms, and gone home, when I jumped and panted like a terrier over my darling, crying, "Why? Tell me why. Why do you love me? Why do you want to marry me?" when I had it, when I knew.

Arthur said, "I'm not what I appear, Sam. All I know is you are something I want to be part of me forever."

I was finished. This is a lawyer, mind you, talking like this, looking boyish and wounded and powerful—and he was right. I was the song inside of him, I knew that, and I thought I could no more sing it without him than the muse could sing without the poet. We were—picture the two links coming together with a flash—we were the chain of eternity.

What I'm trying to say is that we made love that night as I have never before or yet again. It's not that I can't describe it, I can: it was flesh, it was matter, it was hand, tit, prick, cunt, lips, eyes, breath. It was there, present, ever-lasting, unholy. It was not rational nor was it passionate; it was not even man or woman, heterosexual or homosexual; but it was not selfless because there was no self to be less. We were on the bed and he was pumping into me and I had my hand on his buttock and was crying out and the sound and the motion and the flesh and the feeling. Civi-lization did not fall but only because it had never stood, was a great lie, built atop a landfill of orgasms and purposeless pleasure. I had no mother, we were my mother; I had no father, we were my father. There could be no mistake, no betrayal, no loss: This was love; carnal knowledge; knowledge of the instant, all there was. And for one brief shining moment that was known, I came a lot.

# Three

If there is anything on earth I hate, it is Dr. Blumenthal.
All I want is to be an orchid, and he keeps asking me about
my old man.

"He fucked me," I say finally; insouciantly is the word I
want.

"Did he?" says Blumenthal.

"Every night," I say. "He came into my room and did it
to me."

"Really?"

"No," I say sullenly. "No, he never did that really."

"You sound sorry," says der doc, shifting.

I shrug. "I remember it—him doing it. As if it happened. I have a visceral memory of it. It was what I expected in a way, like a rite of passage. My period, learning
to drive, my father making love to me. It's hard to explain." I give him my steely, blue-eyed glare: I have a top-
notch steely blue-eyed glare. "It's like now, though. I'm
sitting here, you're sitting there—and I feel like you're
fucking me good and proper."

Blumenthal shifts. "Why should that bother you? You're
a woman: you should enjoy a good fuck."

Have I described Blumenthal's voice? It's a real Jewish
whine, a real nasal, wimpy, don't-let-them-hurt-me whine.
It's ridiculous. The fact is, I do feel somewhat titillated
sitting there; my skin warm, my muscles relaxed: a little
breathless altogether.

Harshly I say: "So God tells me."

Blumenthal glances over his shoulder, as if he might

have left the window open. "How'd God get in here?" he
says.

"Arthur broke my mug," I tell him.

Blumenthal puts his hand out flat and indicates the web
between index finger and thumb. "Put your hand like
this," he says, "and slam it once real hard into his throat."

I laugh. "Fuck you," I say.

"No, no, I'm the Daddy," Blumenthal says. "I do the
fucking."

I have to tell him: Christ, it's as if he knows. "I did it to
Arthur." He doesn't answer. "I gave it to him up the ass.
With my fingers."

"Does that upset you?"

"It was wonderful. I wanted to make him drink his own
come but I didn't."

Blumenthal hangs there like: in the Sistine Chapel
(Arthur and I honeymooned in Rome the week before we
got married) there's one part in the Last Judgment which
is supposed to be a self-portrait of Michelangelo: it's the
flayed skin of St. Bartholomew being held by himself,
dangling down, a face and body collapsing into folds of
loose flesh: Blumenthal hangs there like that.

I jut my chin out at him. "He broke my lousy mug," I say.

The mug in question was a thing of beauty and a joy for
about a week. I had bought it with the ten dollars I received from "Heat Winds, A Quarterly," for my rhymed
satire beginning,

"Their romance could ne'er endure,
The odor of his love's manure . . ."

It was a simple coffee mug but had a glazed finish of
robin's egg blue which transfixed my eyes and, anyway, I
liked it.

Arthur comes home—this is about five days ago—and
he's all fired up because he has just been battling an at-
tempted coverup in the upper echelons of city politics.
The D.A., it seems, was contemplating knuckling under to
pressure from on high to decline to prosecute a cop who
had apparently—allegedly—gunned down a black grand-
mother who had been trying to escape from a super-

market with some goods she had neglected to pay for. The woman had a knife, but he shot her four times, and Jones, who is black and Arthur's colleague and our friend, smelled racism and Arthur sided with him and the D.A. had actually called him into his office, Arthur, and made an appeal to his whiteness and there had been offers of resignation and ever-so-subtle threats to approach the press and golly weren't it dramatic as all get-out I hope to tell you.

So anyway, I am so depressed by the time dinner is over that Arthur offers to wash the dishes—with that Philadelphia-bred look of benign puzzlement on his craw that makes me feel he is cross-examining me on the witness stand—and about five minutes later I hear the chunk of robin's egg blue glaze against porcelain and a curse and I know the mug is chipped.

It occurs to me even as I go flying into the kitchen that somewhere in my mind I had always known he was going to break it, known as I bought it, even before. I tell you, as my soul prepared to enter the about-to-be fertilized egg in my mother's womb, it was muttering, "Well, okay, but he's going to break my mug."

I snatch the poor thing from his brutish hands and cradle it in my own. There is a thumbnail-shaped chip in the rim. My eyes fill.

"You broke it," I say, trembly.

"Yeah, sorry. I'll get you a new one."

"You'll get me!" I cry, my hair flying. "This was mine. You had no right: it wasn't yours to break."

Arthur's lawyerly eye notes that I am upset. "Uh-whuh-uh," he says.

"Everything that's good and beautiful, you destroy. Nothing is safe. Whatever's golden, you turn to shit."

Arthur has fished the chip out of the soapy water and is holding it out to me as an offering.

"What am I supposed to do with that?" I screech.

He looks at it quizzically, gets my point. I drive it home.

"It's a chip! A chip! It's just a chip, no more than that," I say. I hurl the mug at him—clumsily because my fingers get stuck in the handle. He catches it. "Go ahead—there may still be some beauty in it—why don't you shatter it? Shatter it!" And, crying, I rush into the bedroom.

Arthur follows me, saying, "Sam!" He sits beside me on the bed, leans over me. I am rigid as a board, staring up at him.

"I'm sorry," he says.

"I bought that with the money from my poem," I say.

"I know, I understand," he says, despairingly, helplessly. I love him so much, this man. "I want to go to bed and hurt you," I say.

Arthur's eyes shift to one side, but he nods. We are naked in a moment and I am on him, pummeling him, slapping and pinching him. I spank him as hard as I can, shocked by the loud cracks but I can't stop: I need to see his ass turn red. Finally, I climb on top of him, dip my fingers in my cunt to lubricate them and shove them up his ass, first one, then two, then three. I pump into him while he grunts. I reach around and grab his erection and squeeze it, hissing, "Look, you like it. You're a whore, you're a slut, you're a cunt. You love it. Take it." I am planning, as I say, to catch his scum in my hand and then jam my fingers in his mouth, but I come before he does, and when he does, I am spent and wasted; I do not want to do it anymore.

Arthur rolls over on his back with a sigh. He stares at the ceiling. I think he is shocked—because he liked it, because I have shown myself to him and I am ugly—I don't know and I don't want to think about it. I am too happy. I feel giddy and thrilled.

He glances at me where I lay grinning.

"Does this mean I don't have to buy you a new mug?" he asks.

I laugh. "Go to sleep, love," I say.

Assholes. I wake up the next morning thinking about assholes: shit and assholes. Assholes and shit. I am depressed. I am ashamed when I wake up. No, it is not shame: it is panic. I am afraid. Something bad is going to happen to me today, I can feel it. With sudden terror I realize that I have a shrink appointment today. I run to the

calendar—Animals of the Bronx Zoo; Hippos for March—
I do not have a shrink appointment, Blumenthal's away: I
have till Friday.

I think of assholes. Assholes and shit. Arthur's asshole—
a pink-brown bud as he lay under me with his hips raised
by a pillow and his legs spread: he looked like a great,
docile cow. This thought makes me horny. I want to fuck
him again when he comes home—he has left for work
early to deal with the crisis. Then I remember: I can't:
shrink on Friday. I don't have to talk about it, I think. It's
my money: I can say whatever I want. But I'm not horny
anymore.

I sit down to write, but the minute I open my pad, my
belly bloats and I rush into the bathroom and have diar-
rhea. Shit and assholes, assholes and shit.

I go out for a walk. It is very cold and the wind is
blustery and makes my cheeks sting.

I find myself thinking of God. God has not called for a
while, I realize: almost two weeks. And for two weeks
before that, I have got nothing from him but more Blakian
craziness. I'd thought we were beginning to get past that.

About a month after he first started calling me—I remember it was August because Blumenthal was away and I
had walked to St. Sebastian's looking up at the sky to see
him and the other psychiatrists flying in a wedge-forma-
tion for the Hamptons—we had something of a break-
through, God and I.

I am listening to him rattle on about this and that and
frankly I am having a hard time keeping my eyes open.
Working on the hotline has given me a certain sympathy
for Bloomie who has also on occassion had to fight to stay
awake while I talked. Still, I am glad God can't see over the
phone because this never fails to hurt my feelings.

God is chatting away gaily: "Moving grim over the plains
of Orfalon, I witness Oouoh—" (The female principle, I
gather) "—birthing from her mouth a snake wearing a
mitre which coils around the calves of Marcodel, and enters his nether regions to snare his soul."

"Painful," I say.

"You're telling me," says God. "His soul comes rushing

from his belly in torrents and he builds a church with barred windows."

You have to hand it to Marcodel: he is nothing if not resourceful.

Even as I doze, I am searching through my mind, rifling the pages of remembered Blake for something that will unravel this and lead us back to the personal. Ever since his "I'm so unhappy" outburst weeks before, he has been up there in the unreachable ether.

"Marcodel must be pretty ticked off about you creating Oouoh," I say.

And suddenly, we come down to earth with a sickening thud.

"Yes, he has transformed his body into the weapon and will bring Death back into the world. Of his eyes he makes the sight, and of his mighty thighs the stock. His arms are the barrel, and his organ he has placed into the chamber of his heart . . ."

I am awake. I sit up so fast my reclining chair snaps up late and slugs me in the back. I gasp and dried-up Patricia gives me a wintry smile—her only kind—from the desk across the room.

"Marcodel's become a high-powered rifle," I say. To be honest, I don't know what a high-powered rifle is, but I have never heard of a low-powered rifle so it's my best guess.

God goes right on: "Yes, and Oouoh laughs, her teeth silver, glinting . . ."

"God," I say, "where is Marcodel now?"

"In the closet, where would he be? And her silver—her teeth—where was I?"

My mind, as they say, is racing: an apt metaphor: I can feel it rushing over an empty expanse, searching for an idea that will stop him before he goes on again and I lose him for the rest of the call.

"And Oouoh, where's she?" I say desperately.

He's annoyed: "On the plains of Orfalon, I told you."

"Specifically."

"Well, you remember after she became a shadow, she sprang from my nostrils . . ."

"Um, I forget," I say. "Tell me about when she became a shadow."

He clears his throat to get his God voice back. "A black spot appearing on her gall-bladder began to grow from my rage into a shadow that engulfed her white skin . . ."

I am thinking: Oh Christ, a rifle. "I don't know, God, old friend," I say, stalling for time. "That must have been some rage. To give her cancer, I mean."

There is a silence. I feel as if I have hooked into a running marlin and am now water-skiing over the waves behind him.

"Well, she shouldn't have done that," God whines. "I mean, do you think she should have hurt me?"

I clear my throat to get my concerned voice back. "No," I say. "She shouldn't have hurt you, God. What did she do, exactly?"

"Why are you always bothering me, Samantha? Why are you always bothering me?"

I sigh. "Because I don't want to read in the papers that you put Marcodel in your mouth and fired his cock into your brain."

"I can't," he cries—it is a sound of heartbreaking anguish. "I can't trust you."

"Trust me," I say.

"Do *you* think she should have hurt me?"

"No."

I listen to the sound of his breathing.

"I have to go now," he says.

"Don't. Don't go." More breathing: he is about to hang up. Trying to attach myself to the sound of my voice, trying to fling myself with my voice over the wires to him, I whisper: "She's dead, God. It's over."

"It's not," he whispers in answer. "She came back."

He hangs up.

On the morning after the mug, I do not want to think about what happened next. So I run the conversation over in my mind, and I head downtown toward Elizabeth's.

"Was Christ gay?" I say when I come through the door of the Lansky-Harding apartment.

Lansky, I am happy to find, is just on his way out to a rehearsal. He kisses me on the cheek and says, "Sure. That's why when Pilate saw him, he said, 'Eck! A homo!'"

He goes out, and I am left there with my question unanswered: Elizabeth, in her smock and holding a paintbrush in her hand, is on the phone with her mother. I stand around with my hands in my coat pocket. I wander around her easel and study the work in progress: a still life—the flowers and Lansky's pipe are posing on the table by the window. It isn't bad but I am feeling critical, and thinking that Elizabeth is right when she says she was born to teach great painters not to be one. I've never seen her teach, but I bet she's good.

When she hangs up, she says, "Jeeze, it's ten degrees in Topeka, Allie says." Elizabeth is from Kansas.

"That must hurt the crops or whatever they do there," I say, a bit sullenly. "I know here the Broadway shows are withering on the vine. Actors falling to the ground—they can't harvest them fast enough."

Elizabeth smiles and goes into the kitchen to make us coffee.

"Do you think Christ was gay?" I call after her.

"Well, those velour shirts were sort of suspicious, but who can tell these days," she calls back.

I follow her. "I mean all that passivity. Turn the other cheek. What if someone slaps your wife or your kid, then whatta you do?"

Elizabeth shrugs. "What's the difference? He got his."

I walk over to the sofa and flop down on my back. "Jews are weird," I say under my breath but loud enough for her to hear.

Elizabeth glances at me, smiling as if she knows I have come over to start a fight but her boundless patience is going to outlast me.

"I mean, all they ever think about is shit," I say.

"I know," says Elizabeth. "Who can forget Freud pounding on the bathroom door, shouting to Einstein, 'Comink out, Al?'" This, she explains, is a joke with Lansky. I sniff, as if to say: So now he's got you doing it.

Undaunted, though, I press on: "I mean it. Did you ever consider shit, real shit, the true meaning of shit?"

Elizabeth sighs over the patter of dripping coffee.

"I mean, when you think about it: shit is entropy," I say. "And entropy is time, the difference between past and present. And time is death. Shit is the token of our death. So are children."

"Children are shit?"

"Well, it's all confused in our minds."

She laughs. "I'm thinking of a mother throwing out the baby and taking the diaper to the park."

I am in no way deterred. "We deny shit, we transform our fascination with it. We say that shit parts from the body as the body parts from the soul."

"I never say that."

"We invent the soul, we deny flesh with the illusion of pure intellect, and then we disguise our shit as gold—we spend our lives fondling useless things: like money, say. Our eyes to heaven and our hands in shit." I sit up on the couch as Elizabeth brings in the mugs. She sits in the chair opposite me and lights a cigarette.

"You're too deep for me, Sam," she says.

"Well, look at the Jews," I say, ignoring the pink that is rising to her cheeks, or, that is, wanting to reach out and touch that pink but ignoring it instead. "What are they good at? Intellect. They're all so brainy. They practically invented the soul in the west. And money—disguised shit. On top of which, they all have stomach aches half the time, which proves my point."

Behind the tendrils of smoke floating by, Elizabeth's eyes have taken on the consistency of diamonds, and I make a resolution not to say what I was going to say next.

And then I say it—casually—my mug to my lips. "Isn't that a perfect description of Lansky?"

It's an exciting moment, vibrating, dangerous. And then I see Elizabeth's face and body relax: it is like watching lush waves of beryl sea o'ertop a rock wall. She sighs and shakes her head, as much as to say: Poor Sam.

"I don't know," she says. "Lansky, as far as I can tell, is

not the Jews. Lansky is Lansky. And Lansky I love." This
last she says with an apologetic gesture of the hand.

I lie down on the couch again, holding the warm mug on
my stomach. "I'm depressed," I say.

"Tell me all, old girl."

"I don't know. Maybe Arthur trusts me too much.
Maybe he's too . . . I don't know."

"Passive?"

"I think he believes that, ultimately, everything I do will
lead to beauty." I do not look but I sense Elizabeth is
smiling. "I even asked Dr. Blumenthal if he thought I'd
made a mistake getting married."

"What did he say?"

And then we both answer in unison: "Do *you* think you
made a mistake?"

I laugh. I look at her. She is smiling. "Are you really in
love with the Lansk?" I ask.

"Yup. Actually, I shouldn't be flip: I have given the
question a good deal of thought."

"And the answer was?"

"Yup."

"Are you going to marry him?"

"He hasn't asked me," she says—coyly, I think. "I think
he worries that when the critics pull up in their black
Roadster and spray the street with tommy gun fire, I'll be
hit accidentally."

I am thoughtful, watching the steam rise from the mug
on my stomach. Elizabeth leans forward in her chair. "Samantha," she says, "when God in this bowling alley bowled
the sun, He made Arthur for you and you for Arthur. I'm
sure of it. Trust me."

I moan. "Will you be my therapist?" I say.

"Frankly," says Elizabeth, sitting back with her hand on
her middle. "I don't think I could stand the cramps."

And so, when I have finished telling Dr. MacShrink all
there is to know about broken mugs and Arthur's asshole,
and how I became the great and powerful Wizard of Shit,
he shifts in his chair with his eyebrows lifting into the

mulch of his forehead beneath the lock of gray-yellow hair and he says:

"So what's the meaning of life?"

I stutter a lot because right now in the therapeutic process I am about twelve years old and find it very difficult to express myself. But basically, I say: "I got money for my poem, and I bought the mug, and Arthur broke it. I produced something—I made something—and he didn't—give me—anything—what I wanted—"

"Does that bring up any memories?" Thus D.B.

"Absolutely not," I say. He smiles. I say: "I wrote my first poem when I was twelve years old. It was called 'Ode . . .' No, I'm too embarrassed. 'Ode On A China Vase.' But—" I add in my defense. "It did have the line, 'A dragon in a web of old injuries,' which isn't bad for twelve." He does not react, so I give it up and continue. "Anyway, it was summer, and I didn't go to camp that year, and my brother had a job and I didn't, and I guess my Dad was annoyed with me for hanging around the house all day. So when I showed it to him, he looked it over, and he said, he said: 'That's nice, now why don't you go get a job? People won't pay for stuff like this,' he said, too, I think." My eyes fill with tears, but I do not really feel like crying so much as I feel heavy, pregnant with melancholy, with mourning I guess is the word. "He shouldn't have said that, I don't think," I say. "It wouldn't have killed him to say something nice. I mean, it's no big deal, really, it was just—it hurt my feelings. I cried for three hours, off and on." And suddenly I look at B. and say: "You know, he *liked* me when I was little. He really did. We were very close. It just—" The tears spill over. "It just wasn't long enough. It just wasn't long enough by half." I shake my head. I am frowning. Frowning is not something one often does, but there it is. "He shouldn't have said that. It hurt me. He didn't have the right. I mean, do you think he should have hurt me?"

Blumenthal shifts in his chair. "No," he says. "He shouldn't have hurt you."

Which is why, if there is one thing in the world I love, it is Doctor Blumenthal.

Leave Dr. B's. Park Avenue. Suddenly, March seems the
season of mourning. Not a bad feeling, really; better, I
guess, than the alternative: playing it out over and over
again, new actors in the same old roles; two, five, twelve
years old forever. For a moment, I think: that's what most
people do. Then I ditch that with an effort. Life is not an
argument with someone else. I am sad.

Home. The newspaper. It's almost Arthur time, and I
haven't read it yet. I take it into the bedroom and we lie
down together. Plane crash: 64 dead, but they are all
Mexicans, therefore I am immortal. Sir William Stokes, the
actor, has also died at 81. I read his obit word for word and
I am convinced by the end that he was the greatest actor
who ever lived and that he would have liked me very much
had we met and I would now be a great comfort to his
mourning widow and be surprised to find that along with
his children I was apportioned a small piece of the inheri-
tance. Did his father encourage him? The paper does not
say. Is that a prerequisite for greatness? Have I been
ruined by a harsh remark—a whole attitude, truth be told,
of envy, competition and hostility; unkindness? Am I
really Clementine: drowning as my father digs into the
great, golden asshole? The paper makes no mention of
this, either. Newspapers, I decide, are shallow. One
Brahman in the mountains of Tibet may be changing the
universe with a single revelatory flash and what's the lead
story today? "U.S. Threatens To Blockade Nicaragua.
Communist Arms Must Stop, President Says." I do not
read this article because the truth is I am completely confused by who the good guys and bad guys are, and it really
does seem to me there is no hope for anything unless the
veil of perception is ripped away, our whole attitude
turned inside out, our cities, our armies, suddenly useless,
dismantled, all of us wondering, "What did we build them
for? I can't remember." Death is the founding father of
civilization as it stands and so why read about one blockade
or another when here my beloved Sir Billy is gone forever—how we laughed during the filming of "Christmas In
Hartfordshire"! I will always cherish his memory.

I turn to the gourmet column: "Taming The Recalcitrant Liver Paté." I cannot cook well, and Arthur secretly wishes I'd learn, though he's never said so. The recipe down the side of the column blurs before me—not tears, just the limits of my willingness to comprehend. I reach for the clock radio and turn it on. The classical music station Arthur wakes up to: I haven't read the paper very well today but the station is owned by the *Times* so maybe it counts. They are playing a very comforting Mozart piece, violins, I don't know very much about this but I can float away with the best of them.

At six o'clock, the news comes on, and I think: "Oh good: information fast." The announcer has that classical music station voice and sounds like a doctor telling you he's sorry, but six weeks is all you can hope for.

"The top story: A Brahman in the mountains of Tibet has changed the universe with a revelatory flash," he says. Blockade, blockade, blockade, really.

Then: "The Manhattan District Attorney's Office announced today that they have begun a full-scale investigation into the shooting death last week of Renée Hines. The 76-year-old Mrs. Hines was gunned down by a police officer . . ." and so on. Then: "Assistant District Attorney Arthur Clementine told reporters he expects an indictment to be handed down shortly."

I laugh. There's Arthur talking on the radio. "We expect an indictment to be handed down shortly," he says. I applaud. Then back to Dr. Gloom. "Police spokesmen are saying the investigation has seriously lowered their morale, which may cause them to accidentally gun down other innocent people in the near future." I boo-hiss. The weather: "March became a season of mourning today when memories of hostile fathers swept in over the coastal waters . . ."

The door clicks, opens, shuts. The star of our show is home. He stands at the foot of the bed looking down at me for a minute, then begins to undress. Arthur always begins with his tie, I've noticed. This is not a particularly significant detail, but it turns me on today for some reason.

"I heard you on the radio," I say. There is now a very complicated, mathematical-sounding Bach fugue on. I pull my sweatshirt over my head and reach back to unfasten my bra.

Arthur, looking at my breasts, looks boyish, wondering. "We won," he says, as if he can't believe it. "He killed that woman and we're gonna get him."

I slide my jeans down. "Goes to show you: good always triumphs over evil in the end."

Arthur stands naked before the bed: his pale skin, the slender thrill of his muscles. "It never does," he says in the same tone of voice. "Never. But we're gonna get him."

"Beat me, Arthur," I say. "Bugger me. Make me your sex slave."

"Oh, come on, Sam, I'm not into that stuff," he says. He looks down. His cock has suddenly shot up like a rocket. He runs to the bathroom for the vaseline.

I am rueful, lying across his knee, coming at every other blow. I am rueful, cynical and worldly wise. I will go no more a'roaming (crack) in search of Death (whack) I will fight no wars (crack) no bulls, I will drink no liquor (slap) and take no drugs (crack) because Death is not just a radical (whap) he is also, maybe mostly, a bourgeois.

So I continue as Arthur hurls me onto the bed, asshole open and to the sky, the eye of heaven on earth. I go on as, greased, his prick wobbles into me and strokes deeper and deeper to the canonic rhythms of Bach, giving me a sense of security and a searing pain that does not give me pleasure, but is a pleasure in itself.

Stroke and anti-stroke, I continue: Death is a TV set. Death is a dollar bill. Death is a Communist revolution. Jesus Christ is Death. Death is the family, fidelity, promiscuity. I am coming and coming and coming. Death is a job. Death is modesty. Death is the vacuum cleaner of the loins sucking up all our pleasures into themselves. Death is birth and love and muzziness and faith and non-belief.

But most of all—oh, oh, most of all, my darlings—Death is fucking me right up the ass, and I love it, love it, love it!

# Four

I am a bourgeoise. I will never attain Buddhahood. Such is life. Maybe I will be given Buddhahood for free, here on Fifth Avenue, maybe it will flash through the window and find me here amidst my comforts and I will be suddenly enlightened but still have air conditioning. Then I can appear on the cover of a book, a big closeup of my face, smiling. "Zen And The Art of Investment!" "Satori Through Money Management." "Things and Tranquility."

What am I to do with this ordinary life? Last Saturday, Arthur watched the Mets game on TV. I brought him a beer and a bowl of crackers. I lay with my head on his lap and he stroked my hair. What, oh what, will happen, I was wondering, when Arthur discovers that I *like* this, that I am contented as a cat, that despite the fact that my poetry is growing more and more radical, is being published like crazy, is being hailed in some circles suddenly as a new voice, that despite this, *I* am becoming more and more happy with the little pleasures, the carving on the scrolled leg of the sofa, the shows we can afford to go to see, the dinners out. What, oh, what, will Arthur do when he realizes that I am *not* his secret song, and never was. I am not even a Clementine of Philadelphia, merely a Bradford of Greenwich: I would be content with *less* than this, God help us.

Now and again, I hear my father snickering, and I rage, rage against the dying of the light. But then I think maybe the light is not dying, maybe there is more to come; maybe it was the wrong light—or maybe these are just the usual

51

rationalizations of the 25-year-old encasing herself in amber like a fly. All I know is that if someone quotes Flaubert to me, that rot about bourgeois life leading to radical art, they will not take his throat from me until they pry my cold, dead fingers from around it.

Instead, I think of Rome a lot. I think of Keats. I used to think Keats was the Jesus Christ of poetry, crucified by the critics, his fiery particles snuffed out by their articles, rising up again to give us modern verse. But I do not hate the critics anymore. How can I? I know they are scared and bewildered, too; they too are trying to hold on to themselves. What, indeed, *are* they to say if their Catullus, with his big balls jouncing and his prick high, comes their way? "Does this mean we cannot keep our winter coats? Or wear the golden collar on our throats?"

No, we went to Rome, Arthur and I, the week before our wedding, and I dragged him up to see the little room where he died, Keats, at twenty-six, which I have just become. I tried and tried to conjure him there, him gasping on the tiny cot, "Take courage," to Severn, the brave, kindly, mediocre artist who stuck by him to the last. "Thank God it's come!" Indeed, I pretended I *had* conjured him, and babbled on to Arthur that this was the little window he would drag himself to to look out on the watery white sweep of the Spanish Steps—all of Rome just beyond the reach of his fingertips and he who had seen a corner of the universe in a Grecian urn, with the whole history of the west taunting him, come out, come out, and see what you can make of *me*. "Thank God, it's come."

The secret—that I even kept from myself for a while—is that the room left me cold, Johnny didn't come to me: the scene of his untimely martyrdom was a museum to me; worse, a museum of old furniture. I understand some people like these things.

Then we went to the Forum and I left Arthur alone and wandered by myself among the ruins and groves. I was hoping to be hit by inspiration, hoping to be able to scribble down some bit of brilliance while sitting on a toppled pillar, like Shelley at the Baths of Caracalla. But I am nothing if not an honest vessel of the muse, and when I rushed to an old wall, pen and matchbook cover in hand, with the line: "Oh, Apollo, whither have you fled?" I got the picture and gave it up. Just wandered amidst the scenery.

And so, of course, something did come to me out there, as when the Buddha, giving up, breaking his fast, plopped down beneath the Bodhi tree and entered nirvana. (You can't blame a girl for trying.) Something I didn't realize until a little later, and didn't completely realize until much later. At the time, I just saw the pillars and statues crumbling into the grass and the foliage, and reflected, somewhat pompously, not too much, on how man's work is just another work of nature, springing from his fingers like leaves from branches, falling like leaves, and how here, in the Forum, you could see that this was so in the marble overgrown with moss, overrun with beetles, the Senate of empire become the litter box of a thousand starving cats: no more, no less, than a feature of the landscape. Look on my works, ye mighty, and fertilize, fertilize.

It was the next day, I think, or the day after that that this reflection had its physical effect. We visited the Vatican, stood in self-conscious yet real awe beneath the ceiling of the Sistine Chapel, our eyes sweeping from creation to Judgment Day—pausing at a sybil here, the dangling skin of Dr. Blumenthal there. Afterward, with the light fading, that Italian light that ripples palely in the sky like water, we were taking a cab to some restaurant or other when Arthur saw the pyramid of Cephas, of which we had never heard. Good reason, too, as Cephas was a complete obscurity as far as I can tell except for his pyramid, a big, dingy affair. Anyway, we got out to look around and discovered that it overshadowed, the pyramid, the most gorgeous graveyard I had ever seen and, always something of a sucker for a good graveyard, I took Arthur in. It was the Protestant cemetery where the English buried their dead in the 18th century. It was one fantastic monument after another— mourning angels, urns, women weeping, the images of children who had died—crowded together amid bowing trees and heavy vines. It gave me the chills in a wonderful, ghostly way, and we roamed about on the lopsided flag passageways hand in hand, reading inscriptions to one another.

Of course, somewhere in the dark, distant plains and caves of Blumenthal Country, I must have known that Keats was buried here. Maybe that even added to the mingled sense of surprise and recognition I felt when I stumbled upon his grave in a plainer, less baroque section of the cemetery.

Keats had asked that only the words "Here lies one whose name is writ on water," be inscribed on the stone, but his mourning friends could not bear the simplicity and added a lot of muck about how the anonymous "young poet" had asked for that inscription in "the bitterness of his heart," complete with a broken lyre by Severn of which he later rightly repented. To make matters worse, some idiot had hung another inscription on a nearby wall more recently, an acrostic poem in which each line began with a letter of Keats' name. Can you imagine? "K is for the Krazy rhymes you gave us. E is for the ern of which you wrote." I reflected bitterly that no one had let him be, let him die with his own, real great misery spoken plain. Unable to bear his "Father, why have you forsaken me?" they had covered it over with graffiti, as Christ's was washed down, like a bitter pill, with bread and wine.

Arthur had respectfully moved away to leave me alone at the desecrated shrine of my fallen idol. As the gloaming deepened, I turned and saw the grave of Severn, who had lived into his 80's, long enough, said the stone, to see "his friend lionized," and then been buried here beside the youth who had fallen to his care through accident and kindness, whom he had nursed to the end of his life when he himself was just at the beginning of his life, who, in the few months they had known each other, had cried out the pain of his obscurity into the painter's ear and so kissed him with immortality.

And in that space between the graves, that empty, somehow human space, Keats came to me; not Keats the Lord, but Keats the man, wavering, electric if invisible, from his own stone to that of him who had been not his St. Peter, but his friend.

I was, that is to say, touched by a mortal sadness: the orphan Keats; Keats five foot tall; Keats doomed, as Seamus Heaney says, to the decent thing; psychologically paralyzed when he needed to find work; one of his brothers dying, one of them cheating him, "Oh, would that anything good had ever happened to me or my brothers!"; Keats hysterically in love, chaste, panicky, confused; hungry for fame: "Wasting his salvation on a fierce miscreed"; Keats writing the odes of April, singing only as birds sing, naturally; Keats, I imagine, all in all: Keats the Beautiful Neurotic. A guy.

Then the rippling purple light folded over me and the moment ended.

"What do you think this weekend, hon?" calls Arthur, from where he is lying on the couch under a tent made of the newspaper he is holding above him. "'Cats,' or 'La Cage Aux Folles'?"

Thinking of Rome, as I say, reminds me of Keats, and thinking of the similarity between Keats and Christ reminds me of the similarities between Rome and America. Greece and Rome, I should say, and England and America. It sometimes strikes me that, taken at their broadest outlines, the histories are identical. A loosely-connected empire built on naval power, a people with a democratic nature, great writers and, I mean, how *can* you tell a faggot from an Athenian?—anyway, Greece, and later England, giving way to this great thump and thunder of a garish yet wan republic, its artistic heart self-conscious, inferior, imitative of the old, dying democracy, but its real passion for building, making, taking—Italo-American yang to Greco-English yin—its canvas of conservatism (remember the speeches of Augustus, all old-fashioned values, and religion and decency while taking the freedoms of the people one by one) pulled away to reveal the pit of empire: wars of self-defense leading to distant wars—"if we don't stop them now, here, then when, where?"—so big, so husky, finally, that when it falls, the known world tumbles with it into darkness . . .

Who knows? Perhaps, even as we speak—though, really, it is too early: we are not an empire yet—but one could imagine, in Israel, a child is being born in a manger who pronounces miraculously, in his first wail: "When I have fears that I might cease to be . . ."

Sometimes, I wander the streets of Manhattan, and imagine I am a tourist of the future, observing the ruins, imagining the archaic customs. Once, when a new archbishop was installed, I stood outside St. Patrick's Cathedral and watched an endless procession of white-robed acolytes bearing candles and wafting down 49th Street from Madison Avenue under the spires, buttresses, icons, in through the massive doors, down the aisles, under the vaulting arches to the brilliantly lighted altar. Protestors stood on the streets with signs opposing the archbishop's stand against abortion, and others in favor of it.

This is what they will see—if there are any of them left to see it—this is what they'll remember, as they look at the jagged heaps of rubble—an old temple of a dead religion: These were their rites and customs, they will say. Maybe they will be able to imagine it even. But will any of them know that most of us were going to work, or lunch or school the day they laid the little bishop in his niche like a porcelain statuette? Will any of them realize that one of us was imagining that she was they?

I wonder if the Clementines have a plot in the shadow of the old manse, where some future poet—some Chinaman or someone from the moon—will stand uncoupled from the suffering of his kind and see suddenly my radiant and human presence trembling between the stone marked "Arthur," and the one that bears only an engraving of an empty checkbook, and the inscription: "All in all, I'd rather be in Philadelphia."

I wonder at the way we expand on the coattails of our weaponry, as if we are afraid to build or discover something before we are absolutely positive we can blow it to smithereens.

I wonder: "Cats" or "La Cage Aux Folles."

There was this girl, this young woman, named Judy Honegger, who played the violin. She was from Boston.

She had a clean, fresh face and the picture of her on the front page of the *News* was obviously from her graduation so sometimes, at least, I can say with certainty, her hair was light and shiny and her smile outgoing and bright.

She studied music at Juilliard. I didn't get the feeling she was Isaac Stern or anything, but I could see her giving a recital and playing in small concerts for a while before she got married and taught music and showed her kids the pictures of her in her black dress.

Anyway, she was killed instead by a sniper with a high-powered rifle who lay on the rooftop of the brownstone across the street from her apartment on West 102nd and waited for her to come home from a date.

This was about a week after I first met Arthur and about a week before I moved in with him. I hadn't heard from God, at that time, for I don't know how long.

I loved a boy named Arnold Long, but he was sort of gay, which maybe, as, yes, I have already admitted to Dr. Blumenthal, had something to do with it. I was 22 and had graduated from Barnard magna cum laude ("Why not summa?" queried Pops) and had worked for a publishing house for almost eight months which is to say I had died and gone to hell. Publishing is no business for anyone with organs. It is all airy men and lonely, bitter women playing tough; lunches that last for hours; exercise classes during work. "It was a Freudian nightmare," I told D.B. "From weak father and cold, angry mother to a whole *world* of weak fathers and cold, angry mothers sweeping around, immobile and everywhere at the same time, like, like . . . well . . ."

"All right, all right. Blake's engravings of Dante," said Blumenthal. "So you met Arnold there."

"Oh no," say I, grinning uncontrollably because he has made A Mistake. "Leave Freud behind, we're moving into Tennessee Williams now."

Blumie shifts. "Oh, what the hell, let's take Freud with us, he's never been to Tennessee."

It was in New Orleans, actually. What happened was I quit my job. It's February. I took $200 out of the bank, walked to the bus station, bought a round trip to New

Orleans, got on the bus with Herodotus and nary a change of clothes, and was gone, gone, gone to the Mardi Gras.

I was drunk for three days beginning from the minute I hit the French Quarter. I was carried by throngs of people, in a haze of sweat and noise and jazz. Debutantes threw plastic beads off wrought-iron balconies and our hands flew up to catch them, empty hands stretched toward the gold lamé gowns. Parades went by, people dressed as Bacchus, as nymphs, satyrs—and they threw plastic beads. I drank in bars, in cafés, listening to jazz and folk music. I drank in a topless bar and paid a woman a dollar to dance naked on my table. I slept in doorways and the police came and thwacked me on the bottom with their sticks and told me to move on, so I slept in the bus station where I could show the cops my return ticket and they would leave me alone. Then, in the morning, I would walk all the way down Canal Street, past the bars, the whores, stepping over fistfights in the streets, my blisters singing a veritable opera of pain, all the way back to the Quarter where the edge of the crowd would slowly gather in about me and carry me away from bar to club to jazz cave, from wine to whiskey to huge paper cups frothing over with beer.

It rained and I caught a fever and so the drunken haze became a haze of sickness. I was broke now—I had two dollars which I hung onto for a while—and I kept opening my purse to make sure the return ticket was there. One night, I slept in the stadium at Tulane—for fifty cents, we were allowed to bed down on the concrete under the piers. The place was just a black mass of sleeping bags, but I had no sleeping bag, and I woke up in the first dawn with my raincoat wrapped around me, shivering so violently I thought I would die. The young man next to me opened his sleeping bag—he was all wild black beard and wild black hair—and I climbed in, ready to trade for a little warmth, not wearing my diaphragm, which was also in my purse, not caring, vaguely afraid of disease, not caring. But the young man wriggled his arm around me, and zipped up the bag so that we were pressed tightly together in the canvas cocoon, and whispered, "Don't worry. I'm a student. Go to sleep." What his being a student had to do with it, I wasn't exactly sure, but I fell asleep against his chest and woke up from deep unconsciousness two hours later, and watched as he rolled up his sleeping bag, as he waved, winked and went away.

I was a little more clear-headed then, though my lungs felt like they were filled with lead. I rode the streetcar named "Desire"—so crowded that I didn't have to pay—back into town.

I was starving and went down to the Mississippi where there was a little cafe that sold these wonderful little cakes called *beignets* and small cups of chicory for almost nothing. Under the green awning, you could sit at an outdoor table and look at the early risers walking by the river—the big river, wide and dead-panned and dark.

The place was crowded and so they were seating small parties together. That's how I met Arnold Long, a reedy southern boy with his blond hair in a crewcut and blue eyes that he narrowed when he listened to you as if he had to squint to see your words.

He saw my hand was trembling when I reached for the last of my three *beignets,* and when he asked me how I was enjoying Mardi Gras, though I smelled like beer and garbage and my hair was dangling in knots around my dirty face, he could tell from the way I answered that I was not your average person of the streets. I thought he might be gay, and I was certain he was kind, so when he asked me if I would like a place to freshen up, I told him that I had always depended on the kindness of strangers, and went back with him to this wonderful little hotel-apartment in the Quarter with a balcony onto the courtyard and a little verdigris mermaid sitting in the stagnant water of the idle fountain below.

I showered and washed my underwear and my blouse in the sink. Arnold made me three eggs and four pieces of toast all of which I devoured. Then, wrapped in his bathrobe, I sat next to him out on the balcony, our feet up, cups of coffee balanced on our middles, and between my fits of raw, angry hacking, we talked. Arnold was a graphic designer, freelance, and did some work with the publishing companies down there, so I told him my experiences and he listened with his eyes narrowed and laughed sympathetically.

"I'm not sure," I said, "but I think I may have run away from home."

"Not cut out for the literary life," he said.

"But that's not the literary life," I cried, sending myself into another fit of coughing. "That's just the point. What will I write poetry about: 'My boss is like a red, red rose'?"

"I wouldn't know about that. I wouldn't know, really, about anything," he said in his soft drawl. "In fact, ignorance of life is my major character trait. Also," he smiled, "my peculiar charm."

"Sometimes," I said, "it seems to me that all American literature is either Ernest Hemingway or Emily Dickinson."

"A charming couple. We must have them by."

"One of them expanding his life until his work becomes a bloody echo, laughable; and the other cowering away, churning out those perfect little things, better and better. The life is nothing, the work is all, or vice versa, no inbetween."

"My philosophy is sort of similar," Arnold said. "The life is nothing, and the work's not so hot either."

"It's all sex anyway," said I with the sweeping gesture to go with it. "American literature scuttles in terror between Jake Barnes and a tightly shut door."

I was trying to figure out what I meant by that when Arnold murmured into his coffee. "Ah, now we begin to get into the area of my expertise."

I reached out and put my hand on his wrist. "It's all right, you know," I said. "I'm not expecting anything."

He smiled. "Good. Then you're in for a predictable evening."

There was that awkward moment that night when we went to bed, when I stepped out of my clothing and stood before him, aware of the heaviness of my breasts and my bottom, aware they threatened him. I felt relaxed and in charge and when he climbed under the covers beside me, I held him to my breast and fell asleep.

I did not wake up until noon, but I felt much better, my

sickness reduced to a head cold, my throat a little sore. I
think I half expected to find Arnold sitting on the edge of
the bed weeping, or maybe dead of a gunshot wound in
the bathroom, but he came in off the balcony, cheery
enough, when he saw me stirring.

"Scarlett," he said, "I'm sorry about last night, and I'll
never trouble you with my presence again."

I knew I was in love with him, had known last night as I
drifted off, had felt, in fact, as I was drifting off, that I was
falling into something that did not even aspire to tragedy
but was instead sentimental, unhappy and more dan-
gerously melancholy than I cared to think. I told myself, as
I looked at him standing there, slim and fit in sweater and
chinos, handsome and boyish and hurt, that it was only the
Mardi Gras, that things moved so fast in that mob, in that
haze of liquor and fever. But it has never taken me more
than a minute to fall in love with someone, truth be told—
and long, dismal months to climb out.

I spent the next two days with him, and we saw the end
of the Mardi Gras together. There was never really any
question of my staying, though I kissed him as the last
parade went by, as the plastic beads rained and rattled
down around our heads in sprays of pastel colors, and I
said, "I love you," and he said bitterly, "Yes, I am easy to
love."

I did try on our last night together. We agreed to try, to
be relaxed, no sweat, no foul. But relax is exactly what a
limp penis will not let a man do. Or that is, so relaxed is it,
so calm seeming as if to say, "Hey, you guys wanna have
sex, go on ahead, it's cool, don't mind me, I'll catch some
z's," that the whole rest of his body becomes taut and
feverish as if to compensate. Anyway, we did it, or something like it, slick with sweat, gasping for air, so relieved,
finally, by that little burst of scum from the insouciantly
half-hard wand that we embraced each other laughing,
and talking afterwards, volubly, ceaselessly, to cover any
attempt on the part of shame or dissatisfaction to stand up
where the other wouldn't. And then it was morning and
we found that even the bittersweet drama of our parting
had been swallowed up, threatened with ridicule by the

semi-consummated sheets, as if our friends had gathered in the courtyard for a chivari, pushing our faces in our failure. It was when I got home after that, after I had secured my job at the movie house and begun writing poetry full-time, that I also started my really heavy drinking.

"Sometimes I think sex was invented by bullies so tender men who made them look bad wouldn't be able to reproduce," I told Blumenthal when I told him, recently, about Arnold.

"Surely," said he, "you don't mean bullies like me?"

"Well," I said, into the breach, "it's not abnormal for people to say women like sex less than men, that it's less of an urgent issue for them."

"No, it's not." He shifts. "It's insane, but it's not abnormal."

"Well, what am I supposed to do? I mean, is the outshot of therapy that I'm going to be reduced to an organ?"

"Maybe an organ and a hand: floating vaginas never pay their bills."

I rear up in the chair. "I think you're being smug and sexist," I say.

Blumenthal shifts. "Smug, yes. I apologize. Why sexist?"

"Because you want to reduce everything to the physical to give men the advantage."

"Why does that give men the advantage?"

"Well—" Frankly, it had seemed self-evident to me when I said it. "Well—they're stronger for one thing."

"In some situations," says Blumenthal. "And in others: not."

"They can rape you." He says nothing. I feel my face get hot. I say sharply, "You're trying to make me say that I feel men are better than women because they have penises."

"Got me," says Blumenthal, and he snaps his fingers: a loud crack in the silent room.

"Oh, hon. Oh, hon," says Arthur.

"Yes," I call from the kitchen.

"Which do you think?"

"What are they again?"

"'Cats' or 'La Cage Aux Folles.'"
"Musicals."
"Right. One's T.S. Eliot, the other's fags."
Decisions, decisions.

I have a brother. My brother's name is Mark. He is six years older than I. The Bloomster says I have ambivalent feelings toward him, but I disagree. I think I am quite bivalent. I hope he gets cancer, weeps because he is afraid to die, then dies.

Mark works in California, with computers: systems; money. He is vastly intelligent, articulate, funny. He makes my mother smile when he teases her and taps her on the chin with his fist like Jimmy Cagney. He and my father stand together with their hands in their pockets and their backs slumped and discuss investment opportunities. Mark calls me "Squirt" and brings me presents: expensive hardcover books of poetry—the complete Ginsberg, the illuminated Blake—and when I see his face, which is handsome and dark, my heart leaps up and expands in my chest with love for him, and with having missed him. Cancer of the pancreas. Incurable.

When he comes home, which is infrequently, he sits in the red leather wing chair, the one my father reads the newspaper in, and my mother actually goes into the kitchen (she must need a map to find it) and brings him crackers laid out in a semi-circle on a tray around a hunk of oniony cheese. His wife, Maureen, usually talks to me, as if it were her assignment, leaning forward on her knees, serious, nodding, asking questions. I think she read a poem once, I'm not sure. Perhaps she thinks I am the greatest rhymester since Guest. I like Maureen, I do, but the blankness in her baby blues when I mention the name of the journal that published my latest, the way she says, "Oh—yes—I think I've heard of that" (Christ, I never heard of it before they bought me), makes me want to lean forward, serious, on my knees, and say, "So what about thighs?" Maureen used to be an exercise instructor before she had Bert.

Bert is my nephew whom I am supposed to love. Bert is

two. I love Bert. He calls me "Ansam," and I love the way
he talks, smiles, cries with his entire body, leaning it forward to say hello, rocking it when he thinks something is
funny, hurling it to the floor like a gage when he is mad.
Even when he says he hates you, you are borne on his
honesty as on a tide, carried away peacefully on the star-
tling wings of the real. I peer into the brown ponds of his
eyes and he seems, in his childish but tender way, to be
telling me that my womb is plugged up so tightly that soon
it will become a vacuum and I will collapse into it, crumble
into it gray-haired like a piece of hollow plaster, like the
woman leaving Shangri-la, or the vampire at the end of a
horror movie, finally coming of age: the price of coming of
age too late, centuries too late.

My mother's penis has plugged up my womb. There is
no entry to my womb but through my asshole. (Thus this
charming toddler. "Ansam. Ansam.") My mother who is
coming back from the kitchen sans assistance from Lewis
and Clark. Who is bending over to present Mark with the
semi-circle of crackers, the hunk of cheese, who is still, still
slaughtering my father with her love of Mark. Handsome
Mark who wins the bourgeois game hands down, whom I
could only defeat through Buddhahood. Who has triumphed now. *Satori!*

Whenever Mark stands up—even to go to the
bathroom—I steal his chair. I do not mean to. I drift to it,
my feet feel tired. I sit down with the red leather wings on
either side of me. The toilet flushes. I tingle as Mark
returns.

"Scram, Squirt," he says.

I cede the chair, the lips of my cunt tingling, my ass
tender and pink, feeling as if I have been well and truly
fucked. A koan presents itself: how triumph over a man
who has the authority to decide whether or not you have
triumphed over him. I dub this "The Ice Cream Koan," a
pun that means nothing. *Kensho!*

He rarely beat me. He was too much older to look back
long enough to know I was there. That's not true. He
defended me from bullies. Once, we were ice skating and a
bunch of big-kid boys made fun of me. I was ten. I had

everything: the cute little hat with the beanie, the pompon skates. But I couldn't skate well, and the boys, four of them, Mark's age, made fun of me, and also said I had a nice ass. Mark went after them on the ice—all four of them—and they ran. Mark went after them like a racer, and then, on a sharp turn, lost his footing. His legs went up in the air, his ass cracked against the ice, his face blank, an utter fool, and the boys laughed. I have never loved him so much. His pride was most of him at sixteen. "C'mon, Squirt," he said, arm around my shoulder, "let's go home and hammer the dents out of my butt."

By the time the fights with my parents came, the long, long fights of adolescence: "How will you live? You need job training! What were you doing with that boy? I will cut off your hair," my brother was in college in Santa Barbara. "Fuck 'em, Squirt," he said over the phone. "Write poetry." And for long minutes at a time, I caught hold of that voice like a rope and pulled myself to the open air hand over hand. If everything had just not been so easy for him, I could have loved him unequivocally, bivalently, oh, with radiant bivalence. As it stands, he is a major obstacle in my new career of quiet darkness, of comfortable despair. What will happen when he meets Arthur? Oh dread, oh fear, oh terror. Arthur may shrink to ten inches, his voice a squeak as Mark pats him on the head. Arthur may put his hands in his pockets and slouch back and dicuss investment opportunities. Arthur may cut him to ribbons with a few swipes of his rapier. What will happen then?

All good things will crumble with a muted roar and forth I will break like a griffin with my mother's face, phallus straining.

"Squirt? Squirt! Aaaagh!"

"Oh, hon?"

I pour some coffee in a mug. I am going to dump it on Arthur's head.

"Let's see," I sing out. " 'Cats' or 'La Cage.' I'm thinking, Lamb."

Maybe he will melt away, all this will melt away like the Wicked Witch of the West. Maybe not a griffin but a child will arise from beneath, proclaiming life with its whole body. Maybe, on the other hand, I will chicken out and save myself.

"Hon?"

"Coming," I sing out. "Coming."

I walked in terror like the night, I lived scared for what seemed ages. Waiting for God to be arrested for shooting Judy Honegger with Marcodel, the rifle. I could see the Medical Examiner digging the spent penis out of the dead woman's neck. "Looks like Marcodel's to me." A trail leading straight to heaven.

I was scared. Would he call? Would he tell me? And what would I do, sworn to secrecy. If only it had not been true, I could have enjoyed the romance of it. True, I felt like a little girl, unable to cope. I went for days without writing, feeling that it was children's rhymes compared to the real world of policemen and district attorneys, newspaper reporters and high-powered rifles. God had shot down a young woman and I was to blame. Maybe my probing had set him off. Maybe Judy was a replacement for me. It was distinctly not funny.

I went to St. Thomas' and prayed. On my knees, tears in my eyes. "Oh God, don't let it be God, God. Make it not God, God. God, God, God."

I watched Arthur, day after day. I had lived with him a week, I was in the first flush of living with him. Well, not flush—more like bloom, a burgeoning moment that would culminate the night of Jake's party.

It was two days before that that they arrested the man who had shot Judy Honegger. A thirty-two-year-old black man with a wife and three kids. He had gone nuts after losing his job in a shoe store. God, I felt certain, was a white man, unmarried. But still, I followed Arthur around the apartment for an hour, saying, "Are they sure?"

"What's with you, angel?" said my brand new Arthur. "You afraid you're next?"

"Did he mention God?"

"Yeah, he said, 'God, they fired me from that shoe store.'"

"Marcodel?"

"Who?"

"Did he have a name for his rifle?"

"Spot, I think. Samantha . . ." He took me by the shoulders in witty-but-earnest Arthurian fashion. "It's him. We got him. It's just a guy."

But I did not feel safe until the next morning, in the basement of St. Sebastian's, when the phone rang and I picked up to hear a long silence. I knew that silence right off: it was God, at last.

"Samantha," he said tentatively.

And I started scolding him. "God! Where have you been? Do you know how worried I was?"

And he started whining. "I had to go to the hospital. I got hit by a rock."

"Oh, God," I said. "I'm sorry."

"These guys, they threw a rock at me and it hit me and I had to have stitches."

"Aww," I said.

There was a silence. I was so happy and relieved to hear from him, I had to keep myself from talking. Then he said: "I missed you, Samantha."

"I missed you, too, God."

His voice brightened. "I got a job, though."

"Did you? That's wonderful! Doing what?"

"Hurling fireballs at the angels of Olagon."

"Hey, there's a growing field."

I heard his breathing for a long moment. "They called me a pansy," he said then.

"The punks who threw the rock."

"Yeah. They were leaning against a car, and they started saying things. They called me a pussy. They said I walked funny."

"I'm sorry that happened," I said.

"So I shouted, 'Rauss, Scheisskopf!' And they threw the rock."

I wanted to say something, though I had nothing to say. Sometimes, with God, I found myself falling in love with the tenderness and authority in my own voice, and hoping he would say something with which I could sympathize.

"That's German," he said.

"I'm sorry to hear that," I said, then slapped myself on the forehead for an idiot.

"I knew a German lady once. She taught me."

"Oh?" said I, casually gagging with excitement.

"She taught me songs, and how to do a somersault. I can do a somersault. She built blocks with me. I think—" He stopped. I held my breath. He held his breath. Then we held each other's breath—the silence seemed to go on that long. "I think, maybe, she taught me how to use the potty, I'm not sure. I don't remember. She went away when I was three or so. She married a guy."

I thought of Bert then, as it happens. Little Bert smiling, crying, talking, laughing, loving with his whole body, investing his whole body in those portions of the world he loves. What, then, if that body were stripped away from him? I thought of Michael, wrestling his way into me, tearing aside my maidenhead like a curtain. What then if behind the curtain was just a darkness in the shape of a human, a holy emptiness into which life could be tossed like a coin into a wishing well, and yet find no flesh, no hand to hand you back the wish. And then again—then again, if we were to reach into that hole, that absence, if we were to grasp some old humanity by the lapels and haul it back into being, what cancers, also, what sufferings, shames and pains would we haul back with it. It is easier, I think, to sing the praises of the flesh into that eternal nothing, to sing and raise our virginity like a policeman's hand. Oh, my cunt, my forgotten orchid, it is easier, far easier to mourn you, far easier, still, never to remember . . .

These thoughts were interrupted by a tiny voice over the phone, a little voice singing as if in the distance, hollow over the phone as if it were at the bottom of a well.

"Deutschland, Deutschland, über alles. Uuuuber aaaalles . . ."

"Oh hon?"

I creep, I creep from the kitchen, coffee mug in hand. I see Arthur lying on the couch, his legs extending from under the raised tent of the newspaper.

"Oh hon? Oh hon?"

I creep, I creep, my hands trembling, remembering God as he was that day he did not kill Judy Honegger. I believe in nothing now, it occurs to me. It occurs to me—quite suddenly—that that is it: that is the light, the little candle burning at the bottom of the darkness of my bourgeois existence. That, finally, was the Poet's gift in the Roman graveyard: Negative capability. "To follow the Tao is simple," says Lao Tse. "You need only give up all your opinions." Deep down, that candle of unbelief is burning, unnoticed, forcibly unnoticed even by me lest I extinguish it with a frightened hand. But I will not extinguish it; I will cup my hands around it; I will fan it when I can; I believe in nothing; I will believe in nothing; I will dump this cup of coffee on Arthur's head.

But as I approach the couch, I have another flash of recognition. That is: I notice the newspaper that Arthur is holding is upside down, that the headline, which stretches in two lines full across the top of the page—odd for a Saturday—the headline reads: ".ecnaifeD swoV abuC .tsetorP steivoS .augaraciN fO ograbmE sredrO tnediserP"

"Oh hon?" says Arthur.

Holding the coffee mug in one hand, I reach out with the other and tear the paper away.

There is Arthur. He is wearing his sunglasses upside down. A pencil is sticking out of his ear.

"Or," he says, "we can stay home and eat each other out until we croak."

I lean back on my hip, and sip some coffee, considering.

# Five

My Search For God. By Samantha Clementine.

After God did not kill Judy Honegger, I became angry and guilty at once. Angry because I had fallen on my knees in St. Thomas' Cathedral, mewling and whining and pleading like the coward I am. And guilty because it had worked, and if I rebelled now, God might take it all back again.

I was caught in a bind, because the point was: If God had not killed Judy, then God had. If God was innocent, God was guilty, if you get my drift. If I was indebted to God for saving me from God, then the God to whom I was indebted was not the sort of God to whom I wished to be. And it's no good talking about free will either. Whatever free will Judy Honegger had had was in a little pool in the gutter of 102nd street. Not that Judy meant much to me, but when a violinist gets killed, somebody has to take the fall.

More than anything, I think—or think now—it was humanity I was looking for, connection in aspiration, voices raised together in holy song. Whatever experience of the mystic I had had—in session with Blumenthal sometimes, sometimes on the hotline, sometimes, especially that one time after Jake's party, in bed with Arthur, in Rome—had all depended on connection, human connection. And if humans connect in religious circumstances—what then?

Now, my parents are Episcopalian. We went to church on Easter and Christmas. The whole business was so hypocritical and ridiculous that the religion had died on me like

70

an old man on top of a whore, and I was determined to squirm out from under the dead weight.

So when Arthur and I returned from Rome, I began attending Catholic services, dragging myself out of bed on Sundays to sit in the eerie draught of the voluminous St. Elmo's Cathedral. I followed the liturgy, reveling in the guilty thrill of a new creed—though Catholicism, God knows, is not all that different from the other, which maybe added to the kick: it was like changing sides in an internecine feud. I invested the symbolism with my soul, hoping to bring it to life without losing my sense of the world, without placing all my bets on heaven or eternity. I developed, that is to say, a theory:

The Father, if I recall it rightly, was Being; Jesus was Consciousness; the Holy Ghost was the world created by the interaction of the two. Each person of Godhead was necessary: Being, eternally creative, had to make consciousness by its own laws ("And God so loved the world . . ." I was riddled with biblical quotations.); Consciousness, by necessity, by the fact of its perception, created the big HG, which, in turn, transformed God and Free Will and Eternity into realities. When faced with Pure Being, Consciousness, *by necessity*, I say, saw God. This was the meaning of Moses at the Burning Bush: faced with a vision of the true nature of being as Life-Fertility-Space (The Bush) coexisting forever with Death-Destruction-Time (El Flamo), Moses immediately demanded that its voice (God) proclaim its name (I AM). In other words (words), Being, faced with Consciousness, developed an I. Professor Clementine, in her book *My Secret Loves*, notes that this theme is echoed in the *Bhagavad Gita*, no matter how you pronounce it, when Vishnu shows Arjuna his true self as Life-Death-Space-Time united, and Arjuna begs him to assume the form of Vishnu again. Einstein also had something to say on this subject, but I forget what.

This was wonderful! I was a Catholic!

I went to confession.

"Bless me, Father, for I have sinned."

"In the name of the Father, the Son and the Holy Ghost . . ."

"It's been 25 years since my last confession."

"Hit the highlights."

"Uh, anal intercourse with a duck playing the kazoo."

"Do three Our Fathers, four Hail Mary's, six choruses of 'Fascinating Rhythm,' a buck and wing, and jump up and down swinging a rubber chicken over your head, crying *'Garçon, garçon, où est le château?'*"

I lapsed.

One Saturday, I went to see Lansky. Elizabeth let me in. Lansky was pacing back and forth across the room with the *Times* in his hand. The Supreme Court had just decided that it was all right to strip-search high school students as long as you beat them senseless first. It was the "reasonable torment" criterion. Lansky slapped the paper with the back of his hand.

"My God," he shouted. "These people are Nazis."

"Lansky," I said, "I want to become a Jew."

"Hold this," said Lansky angrily. He pushed the newspaper into my hand. "Now slap it with the back of your hand and shout, 'My God, these people are Nazis!'"

I slapped the paper and it flew up into the air, scattered and fluttered down in a hundred pieces like a Brobdingnagian snowfall.

A page of the business section landed on Lansky's head, folding down over his ears like a shawl.

He sighed. "Have you tried the Unitarians?"

Now, the Unitarians, there is no question, have the best music: Mozart, Luther, the Vedas, anything so long as it swings. They also have the best sermon titles. "The Triumph of Walt Whitman," "The Holographic God," "I Am Afraid," etc. Also, the preacher is allowed to use the word "lover." ". . . more sympathetic to your husband or wife or lover," he will say. Very promising, all in all.

The problem was symbolism for me—or the lack of it. Around this time, I had started to read a lot of the works of Joseph Campbell—swallowing them like pills I was actually—and Joe—or, as he is known in academic circles, Big Joe, or even the Joester—has much to say on this subject.

Symbols, it turns out—bread and wine, resurrection, burning bushes—are neither important in themselves, worthy of worship in themselves, nor needful of theoretical interpretation or explication. Symbols are living representations of the indescribable thing. Thus Big Joe, as I understand him. In other words, you don't have to actually believe in the transubstantiation of bread and wine, or to interpret it as, say, the guilt feast of the body of the slaughtered father-son: the thing is to feel it, to experience it, through the way it acts upon the network of your personality, as—well, as something that cannot be said in any other terms. Here is the leap of experience across the river of which the water-shy horse of theory is incapable. Symbols—metaphors, parables—are the key. ("He will open up his mouth in parables and utter things kept secret since the world was made . . ." Isaiah. "I got a million of 'em." Durante.)

All this I say because, for a month or so, with the Unitarians, my pilgrim heart found a resting place. The big church on 85th Street, with its enormous windows letting light in through the clinging vines. The hymns—"Morning Has Broken"; God, I love that hymn—the kindly, intelligent minister with his halting authority, the impression he gave that he would only guide you by the light of his own uncertainty—all this filled me with a sense, not of peace, but of nobility, of the nobility of not knowing, of declaring myself a searcher, of humility in the face of eternity, and yet the assurance of my right to inhabit this corner of it. In other words, if I had been fashioned to have a religion, an organized religion, I would have been a Unitarian.

But I was not so fashioned. The symbols got me—the lack of them—even the symbols that somehow symbolized the absence of symbols. I would climb the stairs to the broad, open doors of the church, and as the minister shook my hand—he always remembered my name; I've forgotten his: Goodwin, I think—as he shook my hand, I would look up at the pillars flanking the door and note ruefully that they were in fact pilasters, made of white plaster and capable of supporting nothing. The ivy climbing up the wall was newly planted and, when I went inside, the cross above the altar—a vague representation of a cross made with gold wire—proclaimed its inadequacy. Where was the plaster Jesus? His grotesque agony, his blood, his pain? If the only religion you can stomach is not a religion at all—then why bother?

I would sit behind some blue-haired dame whose family had been and would be Unitarians since and until Emerson admitted he had erred; I would listen to Goodwin, Godwin, Woodwind torture himself from the pulpit over even the symbols of nomenclature—"God, or, if you prefer, eternity, or, if you prefer, that for which we have no name . . ." (And what then: do you look up to the sky, with your arms spread, grunting, "Uh. Uh."?); I would stand behind the blue-haired saint and sing and I would feel refreshed, noble, inspired in mind—but not swept away, connected; for what was I to be connected to? What of flesh was there for me to pull out of the great blackness of eternity that had opened before me when God had not killed Judy Honegger? Was I suddenly to fall to my knees and cry, "Yes! Yes! God is a strand of blue hair! I see all!" There was no bush for me to set ablaze, no flame for me to light it with.

Still, I clung to the church as if it were a piece of driftwood on the open sea. Membership Sunday approached—in late February, I think—when newcomers declared themselves a part of the church in a simple, unsymbolic ceremony. Those interested had to schedule an interview with Nudnick and I did so.

I sat in front of his desk, wearing a pleated, plaid skirt no less, crossing my legs this way, crossing them that. He was so young—and good-looking in a boyish way, too. His eyes so sympathetic. But he was still a preacher, and I could not help but think of hiking my skirt to my waist and shouting, "How about some of this? Hubba hubba!"—an urge which comes over me during all my dealings with men of the cloth.

"So you're a poet!" he said, smiling kindly. "We love to bring creative people into our community." When I only smiled, and clutched my hands together to keep them from straying to my skirt, he offered: "The church paper frequently publishes verse."

Immediately, as my heart sank, my mind rose to the occasion and began to compose:

I saw a ginko leaf
Upon the sidewalk
Gleaming in the sun after a little rain.
Oh, curling globes of greenery,
What richness in your muted pales
Communes so with the soul of man
In unproclaimed theolatry?

"Actually," I said, trying not to laugh, not to hurt the poor thing, "I was more interested in your charitable work, your food-for-the-hungry program. I wanted to join your Contemporary Issues Committee, and I can probably do some of the signs for your Tuna Casseroles For Peace Day demonstration. Also, you mentioned during the announcements that you needed someone to collect articles for the study group on Nicaragua and I can't," I said, shaking my head, laughing even as my eyes filled. "I simply can't. I'm sorry. I can't."

Godbole smiled at me and nodded. "I know, Samantha," he said quietly. "I know you can't. But I appreciate your trying."

I couldn't speak. I made a gesture of defeat with my hand.

"If there ever comes a time, though," said Goodguy, "we're here."

I nodded. I stood.

"You're a nice man," I said.

Goodbye shrugged. "Each personality is its own path into the infinite. I would never try to interpose myself between a fellow mortal and eternity."

I smiled. "Hubba hubba," I said.

So, of course, it was Zen. What else? I came upon it in Campbell first, but within a week, I had gone through Suzuki, and a few other motorcycles. I went and attended a few sessions of *sesshin* at the East Side Zendo and Racquet Club and spoke with the roshi Ono Yokisonyu, or whatever he was called. He invited me to join the meditants arranged on their thin mats, thin cushions under their bums, their legs crossed, ankles on thighs, eyes half closed. He taught me how to count my breaths to ten, to concentrate on nothing but my breath. I sat and arranged myself, yanking my ankles up.

Zen seemed suited to me because it is the belief in direct experience. It is both too complex and too simple to explain but basically it is to religion what therapy or analysis is to your own understanding of your problems. It cannot be told, it can only happen. There are no beliefs, no tenets; only the breath, counting the breath, following the breath.

When you sit in the lotus position, eyelids drooping, the mind goes blank. It is an experience like darkness, or a silent phone after someone has hung up. You breathe in a fairly complicated fashion, pressing in with your abdomen, and soon your flesh begins to tingle, and you feel a rush of pleasure—or, at least, I did. I became afraid—I could feel, like a lump of lead in my head, the resistance to letting go completely. I understood where the Devil in literature had got his trickster nature as my mind devised a thousand strategems to keep my concentration from my breath alone. I would breathe and become intensely aware, and would think, "I am intensely aware," losing it, and think, "Don't think that," losing it and then "Don't even think that," losing it, and then, "I've lost it," losing it again. My resistance to release was like a circle of logic from which the only way to break through is to leap the circumference—leap in slow motion, following the breath. I grabbed the breath and held on. Satan, unable to trick me, now cracked the surface of hell and released my demons. Terrible images arose in my mind: my mother with an erection approaching my father on his knees; myself biting off my brother's balls, and my brother was Arthur, then Dr. Blumenthal; the plaster of my face cracking to reveal my mother beneath. I garnered my courage, grabbed hold of the breath, held on.

The images lifted. Blackness. Solid. Pure. My vagina was

suffused with heat, with moisture. The lips between my legs seemed to be parting like a door, at once inviting and wonderful, and dark and terrifying. Suddenly, it was not just my vagina, but my whole body; and not sexual in the usual sense, but libidinous, total, useless, playful—this tingling, clownish pleasure everywhere. Suddenly, a car honked on the street outside and it was part of my being. Suddenly, my head reached into heaven. Suddenly, my anus loosened and extended into the earth. Suddenly, a muscle in my thigh tore and I screamed so loudly that the others around me awoke and old Yokisonyu rushed to me with his chin sagging in wonder, crying, "*Kensho? Kensho?*" and I cried, "Doctor! Doctor! Aaaah!" and was lifted under the arms and carried out to the vestibule where I lay groaning until Arthur came for me.

It wasn't long after that, come to think of it, that Arthur broke my goddamned mug.

Arthur is explaining his feelings on the international situation to Jones and his wife Sheila, and me, too. We are in the Wicked Wolf, one of my favorite restaurants in Yorkville, and I am having the duck. Jones' thin, very black face, is hanging heavily on Arthur's words; nodding, serious. Sheila and I are eating daintily and silently—but I, at least, am listening, pleased with myself because I have read the paper today—May 21st—and know that the Cubans are about to send supply ships to Nicaragua as a challenge to the embargo. I also know that some women have real problems with excess facial hair, but no one is talking about this.

"Look, I don't want empire-building anymore than you do," says Arthur, "and you know how I feel about this president. But the world just isn't the same as it was before World War II, and isolationism—even pacifism—are not viable options. The Russians are bad people, Jones, and they're not fucking around."

Jones nods, once, like Zeus. "I agree." A baritone: it is as if one of the heads of Mt. Rushmore spoke. Jones is a turnon.

"So I don't see how we can reasonably cede countries in

our own hemisphere without damaging the balance of power beyond repair. And I don't think it's that big a risk either. No one is going to start hurling nukes over Nicaragua."

Jones rears, considers, then pronounces. "They are another country. They have the right to make their own decisions."

"But who makes them?" says Arthur, excited. "Government, rebels? And if one side is supplied with Russian guns, what about the other? If they're not supplied, too, it's the Soviets calling the shots."

Jones considers again, but says nothing. Sheila looks up from her chef's salad. Sheila is a beautiful woman who looks African and wise and wears dresses with lots of hot, dark flowers printed on them so she looks like a tribal queen.

"I think," she says softly. "I think this is the end of the world."

"Shut up, woman!" Jones shouts, grabbing her around the throat and throttling her while she laughs. "I hate it when nigger women speak." Jones folds his hands before him. "You were saying, my tender raven?"

Arthur laughs and shakes his head. Jones is always like this. He is insane.

Sheila is still laughing but she also says: "I really do, though. I really do. I think these people, this administration, I think they think God is on their side, and they're really going to do it. I think they think they're going to destroy the world and then be glad-handed into heaven."

"Haven't you castrated the black man long enough?" says Jones.

"Eat your roast beef, Jones," says Sheila, and to us: "He lets it get cold, then he doesn't like it and he gets hungry when we get home and I have to cook for him."

"Damn right," says Jones, eating his roast beef, muttering around it. "Shoulda changed my name to X."

"X Jones," says Arthur. "I like that."

"And then I thought: why?" says Jones.

"XY?" says Arthur.

"And then it came to me in a flash: Z. Jones Z. Jonesie!"

He starts to sing: "Jonesie, what a hard-loving machine bonesie, Jonesie . . ."

"I'm not cooking tonight, Jones," says Sheila.

Jones slams his palm down on the table. "Music is part of our culture, girl. Don't you try to rob me of my heritage."

"I think," I begin tentatively.

"Speak to me, tender white flesh," says Jones.

"I think," I say, "that Arthur is right and not right. That, as things stand, we have to defend Nicaragua and that Sheila is right: it will probably end the world: if not this time, then the next. I think we can't tinker with the machinery to save ourselves, lean on this argument or that argument, this philosophy or that. I think the machinery is fueled by death and we have to tear it down beginning with our own consciousness. As long as there are popsicles and subway tunnels, or sidewalks or radios—I think we're doomed by the human personality. We've confused the fact that our disease is inevitable with the question of whether or not it's incurable, and Freud, Christ, Buddha, Shakespeare—we've swallowed them all and turned them all into our own sick, doomed selves."

Jones considers. He leans across the table to Arthur and whispers, "Tell me: exactly what is it that emanates from between her thighs that has given you the power to dominate western civilization."

"Beats me," says Arthur, "but she sure took the fun out of this conversation."

"Jesus said it," I say. "He said, 'Unless you become as little children, you will never enter the kingdom of Heaven.' He didn't mean obedient, blind followers. Little children aren't like that unless they've been made like that. In fact, they're narcissistic, wholly sensual, awake, aware. Jesus said to Peter, 'You will be the rock,' because the experience of the parables could only be passed on from person to person, not through institutions and ceremonies . . ."

I pause for breath. Blumenthal shifts. "So how's your sex life?" he says.

This is about a week ago.

I sigh. I say, "What do you want from me, Blumenthal?"

"Have you ever noticed," he says, "that whenever you get anxious about something, you tend to float away into the empyrean? To theorize, mysticize?"

Have you ever noticed you have a wart the shape of Massachusetts under your left nostril? I want to say. Instead, I say: "Yes."

He shifts in his chair. "Some people drink," he says.

"I drink, too."

"Do you?"

"No. Not anymore," I say—ruefully a tad. "Not since coming here. And don't smirk."

"Can I smirk after you leave?"

"No." I flop forward, elbows on knees. "Look," I say, "I came here because I wanted the truth, to seek the truth, and . . ."

"You came here because you were alcoholic, frigid and miserable. And because one of your fantasies started to surface and it terrified you."

That Bloomie. You gotta love him.

He sits there in his leather swivel chair, deadpan, waiting for—what? For me to get teary and whine, "What a cruel thing to say?" No. He knows to whom he speaks. I look him dead in his droopy eyes.

"The question, if I recall," I say—and I mean, the chill is palpable, believe me—"concerned my sex life." My spine straightens. I am a duchess. "It is problematical," I say.

I proceed to explain. "The problem is that everything Arthur and I do in bed seems to have a meaning, a psychological meaning that will come out later in therapy. Lately, therefore, while sex has been pleasant, thank you very much, more pleasant than it ever was before—before I started coming here, it has been, how shall I say, mundane."

"This is ever since the mug," says Blumenthal, may his profligate Jewish soul burn in hell until I descend from the bosom of Abraham with a drop of water on my finger—although, now I consider it, this image from the gospel of Our Lord seems a bit charged itself: the Christian isomorph of "Suck a big one, bud."

Anyway, I sigh again but maintain my composure. "Correct," I say. He is silent. "The act of sodomy disturbed me."

"Which?"

"Both. All of it. The whole thing."

"Because you enjoyed it so much?"

"Because—" dear boy, I almost add, my hauteur is rampant, I tell you. "Because it made me think—when Arthur did it to me—it reminded me of being branded. It was like a punishment."

"For?"

"For the first time. For doing to him what . . . For trying to turn Arthur into a woman."

"Or yourself into a man?"

"Mayhaps." I am positively royal. "It made me think that maybe I had married Arthur because, somehow, I don't know, he reminded me of—" Deep breath, back straight. "Of my mother."

Blumenthal shifts. "Your mother, if I remember rightly from our earlier sessions, had a vagina, didn't she?"

"Quite so. I seem to be suffering from a certain amount of confusion on this whole point."

"A vagina's no good?"

"Well—" I defrost a bit, thinking. "I mean, without a penis somewhere in the equation, there's no way to get back to her."

"Who?"

"Your mother."

"Why do you want to get back to my mother?"

"All right. My mother. Damn it, I mean, you men have it easy."

"Sure," says Blumenthal, "we just fuck our mothers, conceive ourselves and live forever."

"Well, all right. But it's true, isn't it?"

"Is it?" Only the Jews could invent a science that works by answering questions with questions.

I sigh, my shoulders sagging. "I'm beginning to think that maybe all this—this branding thing—it was just a way to keep from thinking about what I really want."

"Which is?"

"To get back to her—my mother. Just a way, the branding thing, of keeping her down."

Quietly—almost tenderly—Blumenthal says, "But she came back, didn't she?"

"Yes. Elizabeth."

McB. rubs his nose for a considerable and breathless period.

"How long have you been thinking about all this, anyway?" he asks.

"I—I don't know," I say. "I think it first came to me when I was doing some, well, Zen stuff—meditation." I am a little embarrassed that a sensible Episcopalian should be caught in the lotus position, but it is, shall we say, dwarfed by the context. "I've been thinking about it since, off and on."

"Ever occur to you to mention this to your therapist?"

"Well, I . . ."

"Tell me something," says Der Doc, shifting some more. "We've talked about Arthur a lot; you've railed against him, sung his praises. But I don't really feel like I know him. What's he like?"

I open my mouth. This seems to be a good start. I remain in this position for quite some time and yet, though I am listening very hard, I do not hear any words issuing forth. "Well . . ." I say, finally. "Arthur? What's he like? You mean my husband?"

Blumenthal puts his chin in his hand and the whole bottom part of his face folds up into a mass of soggy wrinkles. "Believe me," he says, "King Arthur you've told me about."

"I—" I say, looking around—the desk avec Kleenex box (regulation psychiatric issue), the bookshelves, the curtained window, all the objects that have become so familiar to me. I am looking for Arthur. "I don't know," I hear myself say, and then, to make sure I've said it, "I don't know." Then something comes unbidden into my mind. Basic Freud—free association. I wonder if I have ever told Blumenthal my theory about Freud. I do not tell it to him. I present him with this unbidden, unwelcome guest. "You know, I guess I really . . ." I say. "I think all I'm trying to say . . ." I look at him. That old face, that funny, mulchy, comforting old face. "I love my mother," I say.

It is like a conjuring trick—speak of the devil and his horns appear. The words come out of my mouth and they are true—the difference between the word "fist" and being ' punched in the mouth. I love my mother. I mean, I always knew I loved my mother. But now, suddenly, I know I love my mother.

And, of course, at the same moment, I realize that I— the child I was; still am—I have lost her forever.

And so we conclude another episode of Samantha Clementine and James Blumenthal in "The Fabulous Circus of Doctor Unhappiness."

A symbolic interlude. I leave Dr. B's office and walk into the park. I wander blindly, thinking of how I love my mother. When I look up, I am standing at the foot of the stairs leading up to Cleopatra's needle, an Egyptian obelisk. I laugh at the phallic-mother symbolism, though I'm not sure exactly what it means. The needle stands surrounded by a grove of bushes and low trees. I laugh some more and decide, in the name of symbolic courage, I must go up into the grove. Suddenly, I remember that the place is supposed to be a hangout for rapists and homosexuals and I become afraid. Again, I laugh: Now I have translated my symbolic fear into a real fear. I am becoming Hester Prynne. In the name of real courage, then, I must go up into the grove with the obelisk in it.

I climb the stairs, wary of attack. I come into the grove. It is empty, except for a young woman nursing a baby at her breast.

I sit on the bench in the grove with the obelisk in it and the nursing mother. I cry quietly because, whatever happens now, I will never have had the love I wanted as a child.

Ah, the hermaphroditic God. Ah, Big Joe, Joester: the hermaphroditic God, what? What?

It was in a philosophic mood that God once said to me—

just a day or two, in fact, before that visit to Blumenthal—said as I leaned my face wearily against the handset. "You know, we were all once both men and women."

"Were we?" I said, stifling a yawn.

"Oh yes. In fact, it was, as I recall, the male appendage of Oouoh that fell off to become Marcodel. And as Marcodel parted from her, she, too, saw that Death must come into the world."

"A bad day all around, I guess."

"You know." He chuckled. "Ever since then, she has been afraid of mice. She thinks they are her phallus, fallen off again, alive again. You should see her, standing on top of the mountain of Zugango with her skirts hiked: 'Eeeee. Eeeee.' It's a panic."

"I imagine," I said dully.

I guess he heard it in my voice. "Are you mad at me?" he asked (hopefully?).

"No, dear, I'm not mad at you," I said. "I simply miss you when you are in the heavens."

"I . . . You want me to come down?"

"For God so loved the world . . ." I said.

"If I come down, something terrible will happen."

"What, dear? What do you think will happen?"

"I don't know. But something. Something terrible."

I smile. "Trust me," I say. "I can handle it." He is silent, and I remain smiling. Everyone thinks that, if they were to let go, the world would explode in the fireball of their passions. It is folks like Dr. B. who, by convincing us they can take the heat, allow us to reveal that it was only an imaginary fire to begin with.

"Trust me," I say again. I say this because it makes me feel like Dr. B. I say this, also, because I am a foolish little girl. I mean, everyone, deep down, has the illusion that their unleashed passion would incinerate the universe. Not everyone, on the other hand, has the high-powered ex-cock of Oouoh, complete with telescopic eyeball, sitting in his closet, waiting to be used.

My cunt is an orchid. Sometimes. Sometimes it is a bleeding gash, the scar where my father tore my testicles from me by impregnating my mother, and then I hate him.

Today, however, it is an orchid, an orchid in the auburn grass, in the pine needles of the forest floor. I am looking at it, so I know. I remember once a gyno (Dr. Ihatechu, the last male gyno I have ever had) placed a mirror in front of me all during the examination. I was mortified by my ugliness, my rawness. What seemed to be a twisted configuration of torn flesh and dried blood.

But this morning—Arthur has just departed; I watched him from the window as the doorman hailed his cab—this morning, I am lying on the bed with my jeans on the floor and my t-shirt pushed up to my neck to bare my breasts, and I am holding the mirror, a rectangular hand mirror for eyebrow work, between my legs. I am watching my fingers fiddle with the lips—the petals, and the rose curves, and the clitoris in its comic-yet-ceremonial pink-brown cowl, and the black gap, the open pit of it, the emptiness that blooms inside me like the doorway to eternity, only it is not the doorway to eternity, it is my vagina, because I am not Woman, I am Sam, not the Eternal Feminine—because I have my own mother, my own Eternal beckoning to me from the dark recesses of life-and-death; and my problems are not the problems of the universe—thank you very much, MacBlume—they are mine, all mine, my problems, my past, my mangled history, and I love them even as I mourn.

My cunt is an orchid. I am sure of it, because *I* am holding the mirror.

But flesh, my children—ooh, I dip my finger in deep and bring it out wet to massage my clit—flesh, my darlings, is only the vocabulary of life—that is the lesson for today, I think. Cunts and cocks and breasts and anuses and flesh are the ways in which we children speak. The illusion that I could ever have worked my way back into my mother is only the illusion that I could be born of myself, eternal and recurrent. If I were "healthy," I would become my mother and love myself, live through Arthur and depend upon him, his cock, to fuel my self-love. I would take his cock into me, into me, into me—my finger is his cock now, kissing the clit—and then I would capture it and it would begin to grow and I would feel the self-love of motherhood. And when that child was born I would crush it to me to maintain the illusion of life—all my conscious care overthrown by the need of not dying, I would crush it to me.

But the world is an illusion nestled in an illusion—the illusion that we need not die, need not love death and life as one. And I am not healthy, I *will* not be healthy because slowly, slowly, slowly I am becoming sane.

I watch my fingers in the mirror as the petals of my cunt flow and close around them like water. I am not masturbating—I am making love to myself.

But I do not come. Damn it, I'm breathless, but I cannot come. How all orgasms do inform against me! Now, I am thinking of a man, of Arthur; now of Jones, now of a blues singer I saw on the street.

Oh, but what's the point. They are all one. They are all Dr. Blumenthal. Oh, Doctor, Doctor. (Jimbo? Jim?) Talk dirty to me, Doc. Tell me I'm conflicted. That's it. Force me, baby: make me turn verbs into adjectives. Do it. Tell me I have to resolve some issues—God, it's meaningless, but I love it! Strip me, Doctor. Strip me of the only power I have left: the power of words. Tell me my head is in a bad place, put it in a bad place, oh, God, I want my head in a bad place. Ambivalence! Id, say Id to me. Ego—oh—oh—oh!

Mind-fuck me, you maniac!

Oh, Jesus!

Oh, shit. I'm in love with my therapist.

After dinner, we put Jones and Sheila in a cab. Jones, that is to say, stands in the middle of the street, screaming, "Hail me a taxi to SALVATION!" until some reckless idiot actually pulls over. As they get in the back, Jones waves to us and then pounces on his wife and they begin necking feverishly. The last thing I hear before the cab pulls away is Jones' plaintive, "I'm hungry, man. That roast beef was *cold.*"

Arthur and I walk across 80th to Fifth with the massive

white facade of the Metropolitan Museum of Art gleaming before us. I take Arthur's arm and lean against his shoulder. It is a difficult way to walk and he wriggles free and puts his arm around me. It is fine May weather—all warm and sad and wistful.

I look up at his profile. Handsome, boyish, controlled, worldly; complete.

"Arthur?" I say.

"Yes, my turtledove."

"Can I ask you a question?"

He laughs. "No."

"Were you a happy child?"

Arthur glances at me, one eyebrow raised as if he is surprised. "Well," he says, "I was a relatively happy child. That is, being a child, you know, isn't easy. Being an adult isn't easy. But my folks—I don't know—they were very— nice to me. A lot of my friends, you know, their parents expected things of them—prep school, the old alma mater, law school or whatever. A lot of my friends went down the drain in the sixties, you know, like history showed them a bit of daylight so, you know, they dodged past their folks— and then, went through the hole and just found themselves tumbling through the air. My parents, I don't know, they were just on my side all the time, no matter what I wanted to do. I remember wanting to be a folk singer at one point—I was fourteen—and my father just went out and bought me a guitar for Christmas. I didn't want to be a folk singer, I just wanted to see what he'd say. He said something like, 'This Dylan chap has a few nice tunes, hey?' and bought me a guitar."

My mouth falls open. "Chester?" I say. "Chester said that?"

He laughs with affection for his father, and I am so envious of him I could weep. "For three weeks, my mother went off to her clubs and meetings, singing 'Blowin' In The Wind,' and proudly telling her cringing friends that her son was going to be a folk singer 'just like that nice Zimmerman boy.' I guess they figured they were lucky I didn't want to be an astronaut—how would they have gotten the rocket ship under the tree?"

"And so you just happened to want to be a lawyer like your dad?"

"Oh, no, no." He laughs—and he does sound a little like Chester, at that. "That took a while. That's a long story how that happened."

"You mean, you didn't go right to law school?" This, I am ashamed to say, had never occurred to me.

"Oh, gee, no," says Arthur—my husband of five months, mind you, almost six. "That's a long story."

I wait but he just walks, looking ahead, his arm around me, and suddenly I feel sort of small. In my small voice, I ask, "Will you tell it to me?"

And he looks down at me and smiles as if I am the same size as ever. "Sure, Sam," he says. "You're my wife: I'll tell you anything you want to know." I am an inch—an inch tall. "I went to Princeton, you know, I sort of—mucked about as they say. Majored in history, minored in art history—you know, I could draw, I was always good at drawing."

"I didn't . . ." know that, I'm about to say, but I stumble over it and he goes past me.

"So when I got out, I didn't know what I wanted to do. I joined the Peace Corps."

"What?" I say this loudly enough to shatter his ear drums, but he answers calmly.

"Yeah, it was the going thing for guilty rich kids. Change the world before you inherit it."

I am about to read my dear husband the riot act. He has never told me this, that he was in the Peace Corps. For all I know, he could have been in Africa.

"They sent me to Africa," he says.

Before I can start to scream at him, we reach our building and there is our doorman and we are smiling, arm in arm. Night, Mr. Clementine, Mrs. Clementine.

Upstairs, I make him a nightcap, but I also make him stay in the kitchen with me where I can keep my eye on him. He goes on.

"So—it was pretty bad, we saw some bad things over there, Jones and me."

"Jones was there?"

"Yeah, that's where I met him. He was having the 'black experience.' He told me that and I told him to take two aspirins and call me in the morning. We got to be friends."

"So how come—" I say, handing him his drink, belligerent hand on jutted hip—"how come you guys don't sit around of an evening and tell old stories about Africa and the Raj or something?"

He shrugs, sips. "Sometimes we do. Sometimes, at work, one of us'll be reminded of something. It was pretty rough, we had a pretty rough time over there."

We adjourn to the bedroom. I sit on the bed with my legs crossed under me. Arthur props himself against the window sill.

"So, anyway, after that . . ." he says.

"Wait a minute: not after that. That. Tell me that." I am not smiling.

Arthur peers deeply into his bourbon, his forelock falling, if I may say so, at a rakish angle. He grimaces. "There was a famine. Lot of kids—we lost a lot of kids. We had to help the medical personnel—there were a lot of kids, women, men, just bones and flesh—well, you've seen it in the papers. But—I like kids, and Jones—well, you know Jones and his kid."

I do know Jones and his son. They're a sketch. They're wonderful.

"So, anyway, the thing is, one day, we hear there's a cholera epidemic in a village nearby . . ." He looks up at the ceiling with a bitter smile. "Jesus. Fucking cholera, it's the dark ages.

"So, it's a couple of hours by truck over bad roads, but they need supplies—intravenous stuff and medicine, so they sent me with the truck . . ."

"Stop it, Arthur," I bark at him. "They don't *send* you on trips like that."

He holds up a hand. "Okay, Sam, you're right. Sorry. I volunteered. I took the truck. I stayed a few days to make sure they knew how to use everything. Jesus, they were dying so fast we had to pile them up in layers in the ditches."

"Oh, Arthur . . ."

"Yeah, right, so, I don't know what I did, I must've done something stupid, drunk the water, I don't know. I'm halfway back, in the middle of nowhere; I got a fucking jungle all around me, and suddenly, I'm puking and shitting and God, it was terrible."

I bow my face into my hands.

"So I went on a while, and then I got feverish and I couldn't drive. I'm delerious. I get out of the truck and start wandering around; I'm laughing sometimes; I don't know where I am. Finally, I fetched myself up against a tree. I'm in the jungle, I'm covered with shit and vomit and this horrible kind of, like, puss and blood mixed together, so I just sat down against the tree and thought: So long."

I raise my face to look at him, my mouth set, my eyes swimming. There he is, my dapper Artie. He goes right on.

"But, seriously, folks: I knew I was gone. I had the only truck, night's falling—I mean, they knew I was supposed to be back, I'd radioed, but there's no way anyone's coming out in that jungle in the middle of the night on foot. Mostly, I think I was hoping I'd go before the animals came out. I was having this horrible fantasy of having to sit there helplessly and watch while some panther or something made a meal out of my leg. I did have—" He looks at what at this point is my grim visage and smiles pleasantly. "I did have a moment of clarity out there, though, one of those things they say you have when you're gonna die. I just saw everything, and it was okay, you know. I wasn't scared. It was all right. And I just sort of sat there peacefully, thinking, 'You know, I'd have liked to have been a painter.'" He shrugs. "Then I died."

"Arthur!"

"No, what really happened was actually funnier. I passed out, and the next time I look up, I'm staring into this huge, bright white light—I thought maybe it was the band of angels coming for to carry me home, but no such luck. It's a flashlight. It's Jones." He shakes his head. "Indiana fucking Jones, man. He's got his shirt all torn up, he's got about forty-seven canteens strapped over his chest. And in his hand, he's got this humungous fucking machete, and he's pounding on his bare chest and laughing and screaming at me, '*This* is the fucking black experience! Now, let's get outta here fore we get eaten by some kinda creature or something!'"

I laugh, even though I am furious, because this is Jones. (Later, when I thank him for rescuing Arthur, he says, "Wouldn't leave you lonely, iv'ry thighs.")

Now, Arthur drinks and I can barely open my teeth wide enough to say, "So you came back and went to law school."

"No, are you joking? I went to Italy." And when I look at him blankly: "I had to become a painter, remember. I had to be true to my jungle vision. The clarity was gone and the only part I could remember was about being a painter, so I went to Rome."

"Rome?" I say, lips atremble. "*Our* Rome?"

He cannot meet my eyes. "Yeah. I guess your shrink would have a field day with that. But I was only there three months. Up in a garret most of the time, painting ruins, good God. Growing a beard. Jesus, I thought I was good. I used to step back from some of those canvases and think: 'Jesus, Arthur, you're good!' My poor mother was probably going around to her bridge clubs telling her friends her son was going to be a painter 'like that nice Angelo boy.'" He waves his hand. "So, after a while, I went to this guy there, Rossi, supposed to be the big mucka-muck: Well, he was. Showed him my canvases. Somerset Maugham, right? He says to me—I can't do Italian accents, but he says, 'My friend, I like you very much. You are a good man. You are a bad painter, but you are a good man.' Of course, the minute he said it, I knew he was right. I was awful. Aaw-ful!" He smiles a slightly pained smile. He nods. "*Then* I went to law school," he says. He drinks. "Like that nice Darrow boy."

I am off the bed, standing before him, hands on hips, my face, I can feel it, red with fury and coming tears.

"Arthur!" I say, "why don't you paint anymore?"

He makes a little gesture with his hand. "Ah—I sketch a little."

"Show me."

"No, it's just . . ."

"Show me, Arthur!"

He heaves your basic heavy sigh of resignation, sets down his drink and goes to his briefcase which is on the floor next to the bed. He takes out his yellow legal pad and flips through the pages. He smiles at the page before him.

"I executed this masterpiece during that hearing last week." And he hands it to me and, of course, it is me, in pencil, all flowing hair and sparkling eyes and a smile like an angel from heaven.

I stand there with the legal pad, trembling and crying.

"You know, it's funny," says Arthur. "You don't really trust me very much."

"Me?" I manage to sputter. "Me?"

"Yeah, I can see it. You keep thinking: Any day now, Arthur is going to creep into the bedroom at night and turn me into his little wifey, all—I don't know, bourgeoise and uncreative and servile: whatever. It's like you think I'm your mother or something. When all along," he says, as I practically reel, "all along the whole point was that I knew you were the real thing the minute I set eyes on you. I mean, you know, it's not like I married you for your talent or anything—you're a poet all the way through, in every part of you. Your soul: I married you for your soul. Soul-wise, old sport," says Arthur, "I figure you're going places I'll never even see unless I toddle back to the jungle and get cholera again. I figure the smarter move is just to love you—make it so there's only one soul between us sort of. I don't know, look, if it doesn't work, if to keep the thing alive, you have to blow . . ." He shrugs. "It'll break my heart, but maybe the brownie points'll take me to heaven."

I can't stand it. I'm weeping. I spin around and march away from him, across the room. I spin around again, pointing my finger at him, shouting, "God damn it, Arthur! God damn it! We've been married for six god-damned months. Why didn't you tell me? Why the fuck didn't you tell me?"

For the first time since I have known him—since we have been together—since we have been—sharing living quarters—for the first time, Arthur's eyes fill with tears—I *see*

Arthur's eyes fill with tears. He runs his hand up through his hair and shakes his head. He doesn't cry—I guess because he's a man or something—but he has to fight it. For all that, he looks at me steadily.

"You never asked me, Sam," he says. He frowns, shakes his head again. "Nah," he says. "You never asked me."

"Oh . . ." His pad, his picture of me, of that ideal creature, falls from my hand, drops to the floor. "Oh, Arthur," I say, crying. I lift up my arms. "Come here. Come to me, baby," I whisper. "Come to Mama."

# Six

I have always been something of an autodidact—is that how you spell it? I mean, despite my seven sisters' cum laude Jesus, oh cum, education, most of what I know I taught myself—or that is, I taught myself, and Jerry taught me.

It's not that my parents discouraged reading, it's that they only encouraged it in the abstract. Reading—with the capital R, was wonderful. Books, on the other hand, were a waste of time. Whenever my mother saw me reading one, she would say, "Practising for a hospital stay?" When my father saw me, he would say, "What's the matter? No one hiring after school workers?" I began to feel guilty—not about reading, but about my legs draped over the leg of the chair, the stillness, the non-workingness of my body. I could not figure out a way to read and be in motion at the same time, and so eventually, while I did not give it up, I read only books that could be considered work, and so got nothing out of them.

Grades, however, were a different matter. You were supposed to get good grades in my family, and the only time I can remember my parents showing any pride in me was when I got a good grade on something I hadn't studied: When, that is, I managed to achieve something without learning anything.

If you can write well, this is a breeze, especially in college English courses. The trick is this: when you write essays, stay on the offensive. Attack. Contradict. If you can manage to say, "I think Dickens is really overrated," you will get straight A's and never have to read *David Copperfield*. Of course, you may also never *get* to read *David Copperfield*, but think of the money you'll save.

Say it airily ("My approach to the work may preclude an overview of the book's themes, but at the same time, the irrelevance of the plot should be self-evident."); stick with all the prof's interpretations even while keeping him on the defensive for his slavish agreement with prevailing trends ("While Twain does manage to maintain his running parallel between the Mississippi and the flow of lifetime, to call this work great is merely to reiterate . . ."); and, above all, *don't like it.* ("Shakespeare? Ha!")

My masterpiece in this line concerned, coincidentally enough, Blake's "Visions of the Daughters of Albion," which I was supposed to read for a class entitled, "Poetry and the Visual Arts," that I took at Columbia. The essay question on the midterm was, "Measure the direct effect of Blake's 'Visions of the Daughters of Albion' on the works of the pre-Raphaelite painters." The problem was that all I knew about Blake was that he was both a poet and an engraver, and I hadn't the foggiest notion of whether "Visions" was a poem, an engraving, or what. Added to this was the fact that I had been mouthing off about Blake pretty steadily in class ("The man was clearly a lunatic—I think the fact that English professors don't understand him has kept him alive far too long.") in order to so impress the professor—Ronald Kessler, his name was— that even if my total ignorance should reveal itself, he would not believe it. Ignominy was in the wings, waiting for its cue.

The challenge lay before me. Other students taking the test had lowered their heads in tears, and one woman had read the question, handed in a blank blue book and strode proudly out the door to break down in the hall. Ronald, all agreed, was a pisser. I, however, waded in.

"It is not so much the totality of Blake's 'Visions' we need consider in comparing it to the pre-Raphaelites (whoever they were) as the specific images and (get this) the general sweep of the lines." And I was off to the races.

About a week later, I am sitting on the steps of Low

Library, under the statue of Alma Mater enthroned no less, and watching spring come, when a tall, thin young man in faded jeans and plaid shirt, with great black beard and soulful brown eyes, sits down beside me.

"Excuse me," says he, "are you Samantha Bradford?" I am. "Well, I just want to tell you that I think you may be a genius. I'm sorry—" He held out his hand. "I'm Jerry Berkowitz, Kessler's teaching assistant." My hand lies limp in his, as he says: "You just got a B-plus on your midterm."

I rock my head back and forth modestly. "Oh—well," I say.

"Yeah," says Jerry. "I mean, that you could do that without even knowing whether it was a poem or an engraving—I think that's fabulous."

All the blood in my body rushed to my feet, circled back to my cheeks, flooded my ears, and took a quick detour to my esophagus. I said, "Then, why . . .?"

"After I read it, I gave it to Kessler to grade," he said. "I told him I wasn't objective because you and I are involved in a personal relationship."

Still stunned,I managed, "We're not . . ."

"Not yet we're not," said Jerry Berkowitz. "Now, listen to this." With which, he proceeds to open a heavy tome upon his raised knees and read aloud to me: " 'My heart aches, and a drowsy numbness pains my sense as though of hemlock I had drunk . . .' "

When he finished, I glanced at him. "Okay," I say, "so he wasn't a lunatic."

"That wasn't him, nimwit. That's Keats. That's 'Ode To A Nightingale.' "

"So why . . ." I spoke a lot of two-word sentences the whole time I dated Jerry.

"Someone who can pull off a stunt like you did should be a writer."

"I am . . ."

"Not if you don't read this stuff you're not."

I raise a haughty chin at the quad. "I'm not a slave to the past. I find it restricts my natural flow."

"And I find that's so much horsesquat," comments Jer. "Look, I'm not telling you you should learn this. I'm telling you you should eat it; you should sleep with it. It ought to be part of you. I don't care if you can discuss it—who cares if you can discuss Paris or snow on the branches of trees, as long as you see it, as long as you look at it, and say, 'Wo!'"

I am icy. "Oh? And what else should . . ."

"You should let me take you to dinner."

He was my first love; he was the first boy I ever really loved. And once I was sure that this was it, that he was the one I wanted to marry, to have children with, to become famous with, I would have done anything to please him, to make him smile at me.

He smiled at me when I read the classics. Dickens, as it turned out, was not overrated, and Blake, forsooth, was the single sanest man who ever trod the earth. And Keats—oh, Keats; oh, my Johnny boy: I think one of the happiest moments of my life—one of the *only* happy moments of my life before the advent of der Blumenthal, was the night Jerry fucked me while I lay on my stomach and read "Ode On A Grecian Urn" for the very first time. I did not understand it then, but the way the totality of the visions rocked in and out of me so gently, the way the sweep of the lines caressed my bottom and my thighs, and the specific images gripped me by the shoulders for the conclusion—well, I knew what poetry was that night, I tell you. It was the first orgasm I had ever had outside of masturbation, one of the only orgasms I ever had before St. Blumenthal touched me and made me whole. It hit me right about "More happy love," and carried me in little waves clear to "Beauty is Truth." And the best thing was that, after I had gotten myself stimulated enough for him to enter me, I hardly had to think of being branded at all.

Mostly with Jerry, I fear, it was all make-believe, to please him: crying oh, oh, oh, oh, while thinking, "Don't brand me, memsahib," just to keep from drying up on him like an old well. I told myself it didn't matter: it was a spiritual love; women's sexual feelings are less urgent, less physical than men's. "Go!"—cried Blake's Enitharmon while I cringed—"and tell the Human Race that Woman's love is Sin!" But I did love him in my fashion, and by the time he left me, western literature lay curled within my womb like the fetus of my own future creations.

I fear I blame my mother for ending the romance. She

hated Jerry from the minute she saw him and, when my mother hates you, it is like trying to function with a steady current of electricity running through your ears. Jerry knew he was up against a harridan, and he loved me and was determined to oppose her, but I think that, after a while, it just wore him down.

It was, not to put too fine a point on it, his masculinity that offended her. He was a very manly man and there was something witty and rock hard down deep in those soulful eyes of his. It reminded me of that scene in the movie "Lawrence of Arabia," when Peter O'Toole is called insubordinate and replies, "Oh no—it's just my manner, sir." Jerry had fuck-you eyes.

She hated him, my mother. She called him scum. She said, "He's the take-you-and-goodbye type, I know him." She even said, "What else does a brilliant boy like that want with you?" And once, she threw a glass across the room and screamed, "I *hate* him!" This was the first summer we were together, when Jerry would come to pick me up in his Kharmen Ghia and we would drive to his apartment in the city and I would stay all night, trying hard not to think about the morning, about walking into the house again, guilty and happy, to find her waiting there.

I think what finally tore it was the time Jerry brought me home at four o'clock in the morning. We snuck in quietly, but she was there, bathrobed, red-eyed, a dragon in a web of old injuries. She ignored him, stepped up to me and said, "Whore!" and raised her hand to slap my face. Jerry stepped between us, his arms at his sides, and just stared at her silently with those brown, damp, soulful, fuck-you eyes. And her hand fell, and she went to bed and I knew I would never stop loving him, and I don't suppose I ever have.

Sometime during my final year, my father phoned me and told me that he and my mother would not pay for my college education if I was going to "waste my time" in school.

"Fine," I said, quite truthfully, "I'm getting my education from Jerry, anyway. He's already asked me to move in with him."

They did not cut off my tuition—though my living

funds were always a few weeks late after that.

They did, finally, as graduation approached and I guess
they began to panic, announce that they were cutting me
out of their will. This is sort of the suburban parent's
equivalent of a first-strike nuclear attack. I wish I could say
I didn't feel it, I wish I could say I didn't care. I wept in
Jerry's arms one long night—not, I pray, for the money:
but for the knowledge that money was the only way of
loving my parents knew, that they had essentially cut me
from their moorings with a single blow. I would not have
given in, of course. I was not stupid: I was not going to give
up a man like Jerry for a woman like my mother—I
thought. But when, weeping, I looked up at him, when I
saw the helpless look in his eyes, the fury, finally, at the fact
that he could do nothing to stop them from hurting me, to
stop me from *letting* them hurt me, I would have known, if
I had ever been in love before, that mother had won.

She had won really, I guess, when she had twisted me to
begin with, won when she had taught me to love the things
that hurt me. No lover can ever be your salvation, really.
Once, perhaps, women could ask that of their men as men
asked it of God: "He for God, and she for God in him."
But those strange, thrilling, unequal, salvific, give-your-
self-away relationships have fled to the hotlines and the
couches—I don't know: we await future developments. I
just know that, then, it was not Jerry's job to save me: it was
his job to love me, and he did. When I didn't save myself—
oh, Blumenthal, you bastard, where were you then?—I
made him helpless, and that was one way in which he could
not live.

Jerry and I moved in together after I graduated. We had
Christmas together: a mysteriously melancholy Christmas,
I thought at the time. But then came MLA, and in January
he was offered a post at the University of Hawaii. He was
honorable about it. He told me right after the new year—
before the job offer—that wherever he was going, he was
going alone. At first, he told me, he wanted to see how
things worked out, but then I started to cry and he said,
"This isn't going to make it. I love you, Sam. But this isn't
the one for me."

He moved out, and the last time I saw him was when he

came by to pick up his Hawaii letter.

He stood on the stoop in the cold and looked up at me where I was standing in the doorway to the vestibule.

"How are you, Sam?" he asked.

And I smiled and said, "My heart aches, and a drowsy numbness pains my sense as though of hemlock I had drunk. How's by you?"

A month later, I quit my job and headed for the Mardi Gras.

"Does your mother like Arthur?" Blumenthal asks me.

I consider. "My mother is sort of—stupefied by Arthur. He's really taken the fire out of her. Like St. George slaying the dragon."

"That must be very satisfying for you."

"Sort of. I don't know. Not really," I say. "Sort of. Arthur has a way with her—she doesn't know how to get at him. When he first met her—before we left for Rome, my mother actually said to him, this is unbelievable, out of the blue, she said, 'So I guess you got something pretty cheap.' "

"Meaning you?"

"That's how I took it—she's very good at making you take her meaning without her ever having to come out and say it."

Blumenthal shifts. "And Arthur said?"

I laugh. "Arthur laughed. But, I mean, like, a big horse laugh as if she had just said the wittiest thing in the world. He did everything but slap her on the back, and then he said, 'Mm, what are these? Tortes? They're very good.' That's the last really nasty thing my mother's said to him, except after we had the Justice of the Peace service and didn't invite anyone. She's still a little sore on that point."

Blumenthal shifts one way, then the other on his chair: a double shift, very grave. "So how do we feel about this?" he asks.

"Well—for a while, I didn't get it, but I think maybe the thing is: Arthur's very sure of himself. He knows she can't do anything to him, in *fact*, and I think he just feels she's a bitch and he doesn't give a fuck what she says. Then again, I'm healthier, too, and Arthur just sort of expects me to work out my feelings about this with you. He'll talk to me about it; he's always on my side, but when he feels it goes down too deep, he always says, 'Take it to Disneyland.'"

"Disneyland?"

"Here. Therapy."

"Why Disneyland?" says Blumenthal.

"It's where your fantasies come to life."

Blumenthal thinks about this for a minute, then starts to chuckle. "That's very funny," he says. It makes me feel ridiculously happy that Arthur can make Dr. Blumenthal laugh.

"You know," I say, "maybe Jerry wasn't—secure enough, somehow. Maybe he wasn't tough enough to win against my mother by not fighting. I mean, maybe he would have been less macho, or something, if he'd been surer of his own manhood. I mean, look at Arthur." And I start to count Arthur off on my fingers. "Arthur goes tearing through jungles and whatnot to bring sick people medicine. He stands up to his boss to get a killer cop indicted. Yesterday, they indicted *five* Mafia bosses after an investigation he did almost by himself."

"Oh yes, I read about that in the papers."

"Front page," I say, blowing up like a balloon.

He lets me hang there for a minute. Slowly, I begin to deflate. I sigh, and roll my eyes.

"So what's wrong with Arthur?" he asks me.

"Well," I say, "I mean, he doesn't exactly have fuck-you eyes."

A passage, oh my soul, to Mom! Passage! Passage! Soul! Soul! To! To! Singing my daze, I make a pact with you, Mother: I have detested you long enough.

It is June 19th, my mother's birthday. She is sixty and Arthur and I tumble into the car, bowing our heads low to make sure our hangovers clear the door frame. Arthur weaves crazily into the middle of Fifth Avenue and we are off. Singing the FDR Drive and the Triborough Bridge. Singing Westchester. A passage to more than Mom. Singing Walt Whitman! Singing Walt Disney! What is the answer?

On the Thomas E. Dewey, we pull to the side of the road

so that I may throw up into the weeds. I throw up in the weeds and shiver with nerves and old marijuana. I sing the body disgusting.

I am Samantha Clementine. Earthy, sensual, sick as a dog. Of Manhattan the daughter. So why aren't we going to visit Manhattan? What is the answer?

"Uuuh," I remark, folding myself into the bucket seat again. I glance through eyes lidded lizard-like at my life's soul mate who pats me on the knee and says, "All right?" then toodles off down the Dewey, Huey and Louie, whistling, his brown forelock dancing dashing on his forehead in the pleasant June breeze through the window.

Hard—yes, hard—to believe that this is the life of yester-night's End Of The World Bash held at our pad boogie down and say yeah. This man—pickled in the case to your left—drank enough vodka martinis to erode the Gold Coast, to make Park Avenue a lost continent. Legal pad in hand, he went from one guest to another, sketching caricatures of our friends in the attitudes they would be in when the bomb struck. Lansky as 'The Thinker,' worrying that the audience to his play might drop off in the fallout; Jones, in war paint, standing in the jungle of Central Park with mutated beasts carousing about him, shouting, "Now this is the black experience!"; Jake, tapping his teeth with a pencil as he watched the blast, murmuring, "Dull. Dull and poorly conceived."; Elizabeth, glancing at it out the window of her classroom, and telling her apple-painting students, "Never mind." He did me, naked astride the mushroom cloud, but wouldn't show it to anyone. He did Sheila, in Supergirl garb, protecting her son, but tore it up. By that time, the party was winding down anyway.

It was a pretty successful bash all in all, the best I ever gave. To celebrate the "shots fired in anger," as the newsmen called them, between Cuban and American ships in the Caribbean. Lansky and Jones, who had never met before, got along famously. Landlord and Othello, they called each other, and wound up crashed together in one corner of the living room, singing the theme to the movie "Exodus," Lansky on libretto, Jones doing a sort of scat riff between each line:

"This land . . ."

"Sit-do-da-diddleothen dot!"
". . . is mine . . ."
"Sharee-ee dow!"
"God gave this land to me . . ."
"Meedle-eedle-booten daten dow!" and so on.

Elizabeth and I had a long chat in the bedroom about how things are going better between me and Arthur and how she and Lansky are discussing marriage—and kids, which Lansky worries will turn him into an old man with no talent, one glass eye and a limp.

Sheila and Jake chatted amiably together on the sofa about the end of life on earth as we know it, and Jake's new lover, Bernard, did a Greta Garbo that had us rolling in the aisles, and Mrs. McFigg, who's a bit of a prig, did a jig with a pig in a big purple wig—I *couldn't* have liked it more!

Anyway, I am reflecting rue-rue-ruefully as we zip up—who was Thomas E. Dewey, anyway?—the highway, that it was Arthur who did all the drinking, while I, with a restraint which, considering the context, was downright optimistic in its implications, had merely a civilized toke or two to be friendly, and it is he who is doing the zipping and whistling this morning while I am primarily consigned to whooping, gagging and the occasional musical groan.

"Nerves," says Arthur, between renditions of "She's Leaving Home," and "When I'm Sixty-Four."

"Die, Arthur," I whisper. "Die."

Last night—ah, yesternight, between the reefer and the booze—when all our guests were gone, he fucked and fucked me in perfect, crazy bliss, his ass rising in roller coaster arcs, his stiff prick plunging, as the pornographers say, veritably plunging into me, driving me into the pitch blackness of pleasure. We slapped and scratched and bit and screamed the two of us, and even now, feeling the tad woozy though I do, I feel my cunt has been blown open, that its lips lie loose and ragged between my legs—that it and his limp cock are conversing feverishly across the imitation stick shift, uttering the words "en masse" while we—the rest of us—cling pleasantly uncommunicative to our simple, separate bucket seats.

I met a Whitman scholar once. After Jerry gave me

*Leaves of Grass,* and I devoured it. It is rare in this vale of tears to feel that you have walked anywhere with anyone. I have walked, I know, with Blumenthal and maybe, through Blumenthal somehow, I will learn to walk with Arthur into the mystery. But I walked with Walt a ways, I know that, too. I remember sitting on the toilet, to be crude but honest, reading "Crossing Brooklyn Ferry," which, for all I know, made me a living symbol of western civilization. I remember hitting the line, "Who knows, for all the distance, but I am as good as looking at you now, for all you cannot see me?" and immediately glancing down in dismay at the jeans around my ankles, feeling the seat burning a ring in my ass, the grainy details of defecation, and thinking a silent apology that he had found me like this. If I'd known he was coming, I'd have been naked, save for an ermine stole, hurling champagne glasses into the fireplace. Ah, sweet thief in the night! But then, who can imagine the Walt-man spinning away, hands to his eyes, crying in disgust, "Oh, Caelia, Caelia, Caelia . . ."? Perhaps, I mean, it was just as well.

Anyway, I knew that there was a Whitman scholar—Donaldson, his name was—at Columbia, and went to visit him at his office. I had this childish notion that a lifetime of studying the bearded great one would somehow be manifest in his face and conversation, would give him the power to inspire hope and inspiration, as t'were. Instead, I found Donaldson a grasping, climbing, bitter, back-biting academic in-fighter who tortured me for forty-five minutes with gossip about who was going to get tenure because he was sucking up to whom, and which was a homosexual, which explains the raves *that* particular piece of muck has been getting in *this* inverted journal; and why the fact that *he* had the goods on *him* had cost him the chairmanship that *he* got by a sudden unexpected change in his attitudes toward *this* . . . Oh God, it was dreadful, pitiful. I wanted to weep, to cry out "But—'When lilacs last in the dooryard bloomed!'" except I knew he would have none of it. I wondered if at some time in his undergraduate career, he had come upon *Leaves* and known, deep in his unconscious, his soul, that here was a book that transcended its good poetry and its bad poetry to become alive and so threatened to make him alive, too; if his destiny was then set in motion—to become, not Whitman's scholar, but his coroner, to throttle the play of poetry into the work of scholarship: to teach it, yes, but always while dissecting it past the danger of vitality until he had walled the great man up like Urizen in his cave. For the love of God, Montressor!

I am going to tell my mother I love her. I don't know why—my theory is that these things go beyond the individual parent, that they are matters simply between you and your introject: that the mother of Bloomenthal-land is simply part of me; that the mother of Greenwich, Connecticut is irrelevant. There is, in short, no need for this particular passage—but I am going to do it; maybe because Death is involved here somewhere, and Death seems to pick his teeth with my theories. Or maybe just because we have walked together, she and I.

My vagina is raw and sore from last night's exertions. Somehow, I feel that rawness, that soreness will be my best protection, my buckler, through whatever is to come. Mark, of course, will be there, too; Mark and Maureen and Bert, but somehow, as long as I can still feel Arthur in me, I will be upheld in this and more than this. Maybe that's what she is whispering to him across the imitation stick shift: "Be with me." And he: "I will."

A passage, my soul, to India!

"Pull over again, would you, darling?" I say. "Quick!"

They are streaming off the porch of the old manse, the old colonnaded white manse, onto the lawn. Mother is pecking Arthur on the cheek, Mark and Maureen are kissing me—I am introducing them to Arthur and exclaiming that Bert has grown and the last time I saw him he was no bigger than. Dad has his hands in his pockets and is leaning back, smiling, as if he is discussing Wall Street with Mark and I have a sudden flash—a sort of sense that he is malevolent, bursting on my consciousness like a firework until I snap it off, reminding myself of turning off the TV during the fireworks titles of Walt Disney's "Wonderful World of Color." What is the answer?

Mother does not kiss me. Mother never does. She

squeezes my shoulder and says, "You look gray, dear. Are you all right?" I tell her I was carsick and, as we all climb the porch and head for the door, she begins telling Arthur a story of how I wet my bed once when I was five or something—her way of belittling me, de-sexing me, but there is that rawness, and then Arthur is cutting her off, telling her a story of how *he* wet himself—his way of telling her that he has laid aside childish things and she should do likewise, and she says, "Well . . ." as if she really has something important to do and disappears indoors before the rest of us and even as Mark grabs Arthur's elbow to start the masculine joust which thrills and terrifies me at once, my cunt feels Arthur's cock giving me the okay sign with a big grin and wiggling its eyebrows like Groucho Marx. The notion of a penis with eyebrows like Groucho Marx strikes me as extraordinarily refreshing and healthy and I am silently passing the high-sign on to the Dr. Blumenthal of the mind as Maureen, Father and Bert surround me and carry me into the darkness of the house.

Indoors, everything is passing gay. There are tortes and danishes and coffee, sweet coffee, beautiful black coffee, my pal of pals, and we are all having conversations which are allowed to progress even to the point of laughter before my mother interrupts with something like, "Oh, Todd Billings died," or, when she has run out of corpses, "Oh, John, would you mind emptying the litter box, I forgot." My mother is afraid of laughter because, I guess, the gods might hear it and—do what? What can the gods do to us for our laughter that they do not do to us anyway? Mother knows.

There are two basic conversations going on at once and I am in the unfortunate position of having to talk in one while wanting to listen to the other. In my conversation, which I have been dreading, Maureen, leaning forward, elbows on knees, face intense, is asking me about my book (yes, well, the fact is: my poems are to be published in a book), and I am explaining about the award (I sort of won the Whitman award last week) and I am joking that I hope it is published before the war so that when the cockroaches evolve into archaeologists they'll discover the fragments, and Maureen is saying, "Oh, but you must be very pleased," and I am disarmed and say, "I am. I am pleased," at which point, my father, dandling Bert between his knees, says, "So—is there any payment for this?" and the firework of his malevolence blows up again—someone keeps turning on the TV—until I snap it off—and I hear myself say, "A little, but I don't worry about that too much because I'm wealthy," and he: "You mean, *Arthur* is wealthy," and I give him a veritably Arthurian grin and say, "Dad, I hate to be the one to break this to you, but Arthur and I have gotten married." This week on Walt Whitman's Wonderful World of Dolor: Minnie suddenly realizes that not all her problems are with Mother Mouse, who breaks in at this point to tell Maureen for the fortieth time that she only has our word for the fact of our being married, not having been invited, you see, to the wedding, and Maureen quips—yes, the dear girl quips, I didn't know she had it in her—that maybe we'll produce the license later, then turns to me, elbows on her knees and says, "So this award . . ." And I want to kiss her on her quipping lips for extricating us all from this ugliness with a California-bred sensitivity which, like most forms of tenderness, is always an admirable quality when it appears in someone else and is directed towards yourself.

Meanwhile, Arthur and Mark.

Mark: So—I hear you've been getting your face in the papers lately.

Arthur: Ah, well, you shouldn't waste time reading the funnies . . .

Mark: Five big-time mobsters, was it?

Arthur: Let's see: Flattop, Joker, Lex Luther, The Riddler and Mr. Mxzlptlk—yeah, five.

Mark: This should increase your chances of running for D.A., shouldn't it?

Arthur shrugs.

Mark: Doesn't that create tension with your boss?

Arthur (more seriously): Actually, I think he's running for Congress.

Mark: Well, then: D.A., Governor; who knows I could be the First Lady's brother.

I spill coffee on my dress at the thought of my becoming
First Lady, but on the other hand, a whole generation of
women modeling themselves on me might be a lot more
interesting than Jackie Kennedy's pillbox hats.

Then Mark says: "Until these thugs are set free on
technicalities. Then the whole house of cards comes tumbling down, right?"

Arthur shrugs again. "I'll always have my membership
in the Thomas E. Dewey fan club."

As I picture future generations of female poets vomiting
in the weeds beside the Arthur C. Clementine Thruway, it
occurs to me that both these conversations, the one I am
talking in and the one I am listening to, are really one
conversation. They progress thusly: Bring up our achieve-
ments, override our modesty until we admit our pride in
them, then cut us down. Mark's apple, apparently, has not
fallen far from Dad's tree.

"So, Mark," I call across the room. "How's the computer
business?" because I know that what is really bugging Mark
is that Arthur is a big-time crimebuster while he is in
"systems" and feels like a wimp just as my father is angry
because I am a poet and he thinks that means I think his
life is a waste whereas in reality (while that may be true,
I'm not sure) he is only projecting, doncha know, his own
opinion of himself onto me, half hoping, half fearing I'll
confirm it. Now, Mark is sort of withering as Arthur ex-
presses the interest in his business that he evinces toward
everyone because he's that kind of guy, which makes me
positively burst with the knowledge, which I cannot reveal,
that one of his Mafia biggies has cracked and is pouring
out enough information by the minute to completely
change the balance of Law vs. Organized Crime to the Law
side, and that I, for one, think "The President's Commis-
sion on Sexual Sanity, Mental Health and Spiritual Enlightenment" has a positively nifty ring to it and that I,
having rescued my beloved for the nonce from the familial
hostilities, allowing him to drink his coffee in peace, can
hear my cunt calling out to his cock, "Say-hey, buddy, slap
me five! Oh. Well, slap me one!" and I am warming to the
fact that, despite my passion for my shrink, I seem simul-

taneously to be falling head over heels in love with my husband, dear boy that he is, just as Inez or Ramona or Consuela or whoever serves the Birthday Brunch.

My mother is sixty. Her hair is cut short now, and it is gray. She wore it longer in her youth. Her watchful, wary, frightened eyes live in a deepening nest of wrinkles, wrinkles written by her fear; and the lines of a lifetime's tension are scrawled at the corners of her mouth. The flesh of her hands is sagging a little, and I see liver spots on the backs, between the prominent veins. Am I surprised to see my mother has grown old? A little, not much. It happened quickly, overnight, it seems, and yet it seems, too, that she has always been old, acted old, like a person effacing herself to keep others from doing it to her. I think, perhaps, that she is more surprised than I. All her life she has paid off Death—or whatever it is she fears that is the mask of Death—with little superstitious terrors, with a minimum of motion to slow down time, with a profession of hatred for Eros, like the teacher's pet sneering at the class buffoon. And yet Death has taken all this motionlessness and fear as a mere payment of interest and is still coming, coming, coming to collect the principal. Had she stolen her life outright, had she claimed her existence as her own and paid nothing—for possession, after all, is nine tenths of the law—had she lived gaily, playfully to the very edge of things, Death could do no more than he already will.

When the cake comes in, I walk to the head of the table, and bend beside the rosewood chair, and kiss her cheek and say, "Happy birthday, Mom. I love you."

She smiles vaguely in my direction, then turns to my father at the other end of the table and says, "Did you remember to drain off the boiler, John?"

The next day, I hear from God again, under rather comic circumstances if you go in for the comedy of despair.

Patricia, across the room, has caught a long one and for the last half hour the only line open is mine and it is ringing continually. First, I get Melinda, or as we call her in the trade, the Rape Lady. Melinda calls every day just about and always begins by saying, "I've been raped," which is always true because she continues to date her rapist, who continues to force himself on her in every way known, so to speak, to man. Melinda is always very upset about this, but every time you suggest that she give this creep the scramola, she becomes furious and abusive and says things like, "What the fuck do you know about it, you fucking whore?" (Fag for the gents.) On top of this, she has the annoying habit of playing her radio very loudly, so that today, for instance, as she is weeping absolutely copiously over Joe's latest atrocity, which, I confess, is grimly original even for Joe, in the background I hear Tom Frankson singing "Popsicle Toes," and I am very close to laughing which would make looking in the mirror something of an impossibility for the next few days.

Now, because of her frequent calls, and her tendency to get nasty, Melinda has been limited by our supervisor to one fifteen minute call a day, and when her time is up, I tell her I must go. She is furious and calls me names, and eventually I am forced to apologize and hang up. Melinda retaliates with silent calls—i.e., phoning over and over and breathing into the phone—while in the background now, Sammy Davis Jr. is doing "The Candy Man": "Who can make a rainbow? Sprinkle it with cream. . . ?" The problem with these calls is you have to keep answering and hold on until you're sure it is not someone else, someone desperate, trying to find the courage to speak. With Melinda, fortunately, the radio is a giveaway—who else listens to that station? Finally, the phone rings, I pick up, and indeed it is someone else. It is Guy or, as we call him, the Cancer Guy. Guy is also a daily caller, who is worried that he has cancer. Primarily, he worries that he has it in his testicles, but occasionally he'll throw us a lung or gall bladder just to keep us interested. Does Guy ever go to a doctor? Surely you jest. What he does is repeatedly ask *us* whether he has the disease or not, and when we refuse to diagnose him, starts whining, "You aren't helping me, you're supposed to help me, why don't you help me," which, I admit, broke my heart the first hundred and fifty times I heard it. Guy,

too, has been limited to fifteen minutes a day (and has, like
Melinda, been barred from every other hotline in the tri-
state area, which we, in our good-heartedness, never do)
and, when I end the call, goes into his litany: "Just tell me
this: Do you think I have cancer?"

"I'm not a doctor, Guy."

"You're not helping me . . ."

Until I have to hang up. The minute I do, Melinda starts
calling again (Dionne Warwick: "Do You Know The Way
To San José?"). And when I hang up on her, Guy calls
back: "Just—do you think I have cancer?" The next five
minutes pass in this fashion. Ring. Lifeline. L.A. is a great
big freeway . . . Click. Ring. Lifeline. Do you think I have
cancer? Click. Ring. Lifeline. In a week, maybe two, they'll
make you a star. Click. Ring. Cancer? Click. Ring. San
José? Click. Ring. Cancer? Click. Ring. San José? Until,
finally, I lose my temper. The phone rings, and I grab it
and scream:

"No!"

For the next few seconds, I am unsure whether I have
cured Guy or left Dionne stranded on Ventura Boulevard.
Then, a little voice asks:

"Sam?"

And it is God.

I sigh. "Oh God, God," I say. "I'm sorry."

"Is someone bothering you?"

He sounds very protective and I can just see the head-
lines: "Rape Lady And Cancer Guy Gunned Down By
God."

"No, no, I just—thought it was someone else," I say. And
quickly: "So how are you?"

There is a pause while, I imagine, he decides whether or
not to let this drop. Then: "Frankly, Sam, I'm very concerned about the international situation."

"Well, we all are, Sweetie. It's very tense."

"I think the end is coming."

"Well—we hope not." I can't do much better than that.
What do you say when the world is such that a psychopath's
concerns become entirely reasonable?

"I have a vision," says God, "of the anger of the serpent

erupting. Of the church of Marcodel's soul igniting into great clouds of noxious gas. Oouoh laughs and laughs at the triumph of Virgin Woman, as men embrace in passion, driving the organs of their individuality into the gap of the endless night. Hero after hero leans forward to kiss his reflection in the lake of fire and plunges into the abyss, screaming and screaming, while the daughters of Samooni dangle from the rotting branches of the trees in Central Park and plead for release until they wither and crumble to the ground where they are dashed to pieces by the acid rain. I see God pluck his heart from his own chest and laugh because it is the skull of man and he copulates with its eyesockets with his two-pronged organ, trumpeting the triumph of his nameless father's rage. I see oceans rushing in over the borders of the land to clog the wailing mouths of babes with the bitter salt of unshed tears. I see no end to the silences of unlived lives trodding the empty air as mourning spectres. I see Carol Burnett with a bucket and mop."

"Cleaning up?"

"No, I left the TV on. Hold it a second."

Well, I think as he goes to click off the set, that's the last time I neglect to read the morning paper.

He's back. "So what do you think's going to happen?" he asks.

I had not been prepared for this, and I falter. For some reason, I am thinking of yesterday, as Arthur and I left my parents' house to drive home. In the dark car, enjoying, this time, the mild night breezes, I look at my darling's silhouette and say, "Do you really think you could be president?"

He laughs. "I'm an assistant D.A., Sam. I think, if everything breaks just right, I could be D.A."

I cross my arms and huddle in the corner. "All right. Don't tell me your hopes, fears, dreams and ambitions. I'm just your old wife, anyway."

He reaches from the steering wheel and pats my thigh. "I love you, old wife," he says.

"Do you talk to Jones about it?"

"No. I don't really think about it, sweetheart. Honestly."

"Well, so, think about it. I'm kind of interested."

"Okay." He thinks about it in the dark. "I think," he says finally, "I could one day be governor."

"Jesus! Really?"

"My family is pretty big in the national party. If I make D.A., if things go well, if, if, if—I think I could get the nomination, and then it's up to the voters. So—now you have 16 million ifs, and I get to be governor. Once you're governor, you're a possible candidate for president and, that's it: straight from A.D.A. to the White House."

I consider this for a while. I watch the shadows of the blossoming willows by the road.

"Then I think we should get a divorce," I say.

"Well, Sam, I'm glad we could have this little chat," says Arthur.

"No, I'm serious. You can't be president weighted down by someone like me. I've got a psychiatric history, a drinking problem. If the public ever got ahold of my poetry, they'd think it was pornography."

"That's six votes right there."

"I won't stand in your way, Arthur."

"I appreciate that, Sam. But it's a long walk to Manhattan, maybe we ought to give this a few more miles."

"I'm serious."

"You're not serious. You can't be serious," Arthur says. "I resign the presidency."

"You can't. I won't let you."

"Well, there you are. I cannot continue without the help and support of the woman I love."

"Who said that?"

"Dewey, I think. Maybe Huey, I'm not sure."

"Who was he, anyway?"

"Look, Samantha, darling girl, light of my life," says Arthur, "I have the mind, the talent and the tenacity to change the world for good, but I'm not going to give up the best blow jobs in America to do it, and if the public can't accept that—oh, what the hell, by that time, we'll all probably be living in mud huts wearing bones in our noses, anyway. I'll have to run for totem. Wo!"

Mouth agape, lips moistened, I have made a dive for his zipper, and he is screaming: "Oh, God! Chappaquiddick!"

"Sam?"

"What?" It is God, bringing me, smiling, out of this remembrance of dingus past. "Oh," I say, "God."

"So?"

"So what?"

"So what do *you* think will happen to the world, Sam?"

I shake my head; sigh; sigh. "Oh God, Gosh—I mean, gosh, God . . ."

"What?"

"I don't know," I say. "All I know is that it's time for a change."

# Seven

"I have a theory," I say, "that Charles Dickens' *A Christmas Carol* is really about psychotherapy."

Blumenthal shifts. "Humbug," he says.

"No, really. It's a spiritual classic. On the anniversary of his death—which is also the anniversary of the birth of the Son of God—Marley, the phantom father, comes to warn Scrooge of the ultimate fate of anal retentive characters like himself. Scrooge consults Dr. Spirit, who at first appears to him as a vague mixture of feminine and masculine qualities that will guide him into the past. 'Long past?' asks Scrooge. 'No, your past,' answers the doc. Off Scrooge goes to see himself rejected by his father, and only allowed to approach him again under the auspices of his sister—in other words, he has to repress his masculine rage against the old man and his desire for his mother, and thus the pleasures of life. This is why he hates his nephew: because he is proof of his sister's sexuality—the process he's come to associate with castration and death. Freud's—sorry, Scroogian slip—Scrooge's masculinity reemerges in his adolescence, represented by good father Fezziwig, and he gets engaged. But slowly, he must hold more and more of himself in in order to keep both his rage and femininity from reemerging. He becomes a grasping miser, losing his fiancée, replacing Eros with Thanatos in the guise of the love of money.

"At this point when Scrooge's resistance breaks down, and he extinguishes the light of his past, transference occurs—Dr. Spirit becomes the jovial, all-powerful father

115

bearing the phallic horn of plenty. Suddenly, through this attachment, the world seems bright again and full of cheer, and Freud—*Scrooge*—can mourn what his life would have been like if he had not been such a crazy by vicariously enjoying Cratchit's poor but happy Christmas. Then, the shadow of another ill falls across his mind in the predicted death of Tiny Tim, through Scrooge's own stinginess—the threat that he will perpetuate his father's sins upon his proxy-son, and so continue the darkness of his non-life into eternity. At this point, he sees to his horror that Dr. Spirit is ageing; that the all-powerful father-God is only a human being. With which, Dr. Spirit parts his robes and, where his genitals should be, there is Ignorance and Want—Repression and the resultant twisted version of Lust.

"It's then that Dr. Spirit becomes the silent mirror of life-and-death itself, throwing Scrooge upon the fact of his mortality and thus an acceptance of his own responsibility for life as it is."

And so saying, I bury my face in my hands and weep. I weep and weep, the tears dripping through the cracks in my fingers. I weep for five minutes and my throat becomes sore from the heaving sobs. Then, with a harsh gasp, I sit up in the chair and peer, owly, through the blur at the Spirit of Therapy Yet To Come.

Said Spirit shifts in his chair. "I thought *A Christmas Carol* had a happy ending."

I nod and laugh, sniffling.

"Alistair Sim does a somersault, doesn't he? Or is that 'It's a Wonderful Life'?"

"Have you ever noticed that those two stories are mirror images of each other?"

"No," says Blumenthal. "Why are you crying?"

"Because," I say, pouting, sniffling, wiping my nose on the sleeve of my sweetest blouse with the maroon slashes on tan which I wore just for him. "Because I'm getting better. I can feel it. I'm saner. I'm calmer. I'm happier than I've ever been. I'm as light as a feather, as happy as a schoolboy . . ."

"Giddy as a drunken man?"

"Uh huh."

"Maybe we should try electro-shock."

"I love you," I tell Blumenthal, and he nods once with regal gravity. "And I don't want to leave you, and in a few years, I'll be all well, and then I'll have to. Damn it!" I slam my fist down on the chair so that the pain goes shivering clear up to my shoulder. "That's all it is, all it ever is: it's one loss after another. It's learning to love something, then giving it up. It's loss, loss, loss, loss, loss. You lose the womb, and then your mother. You lose your looks, your children, your health, and then you lose your life. Everything you hold onto turns to poison and only the things you let go of become sweet and beautiful and melancholy, and I hate it. I hate it. Everything is either King Lear or Prospero: You either try too hard to hold on and you're slowly reduced to nothing, or you give everything away, everything you love and you become a tragic magician. It's an awful way to run things. The only state of mind with anything to offer is mourning. It stinks."

"Yes," says Blumenthal.

I glare. "Don't say yes. What are you thinking?"

"You don't want to know."

"Yes, I do." I stick out my lower lip as miserably and adorably as I can. "Tell me."

"Well—" Blumenthal heaves a big sigh. "I'm sorry, but, really, what I was thinking is that what Lear held onto and Prospero let go of were their daughters—that they were both the fathers of daughters."

"Oh God!" I throw my hands up. "How could you be thinking that? What sort of man are you?"

Blumenthal scratches the pulpy wad of his nose. "What would a real man be thinking?"

"You should be thinking," I say, " 'Here is some beautiful young stuff who loves me slavishly, how can I abuse the therapeutic situation and get myself some nookie?' "

I laugh. He smiles. "So," he says, "I'm either a rapist or a weakling."

"Right."

"Like your father."

"Right." He doesn't answer. I look at the ceiling. "That

shit. Why didn't he want me?" I say, calmer now. "The minute I became a woman, he dumped me like a hot potato. It's like you get your period and the bell goes off and no more Daddy. And it's worse when he'd been so nice to me before that, telling me stories. He had these stories about the people who live inside soap bubbles—I used to blow bubbles by the hour trying to see them—he sang me songs; he was in securities and he used to come home from the office and make up songs to sing me." I keep staring at the ceiling and I whisper:

"'Samantha Bradford, you are so cute.
And your toes are tiny to boot.
And your fingers are tiny to glove.
How wonderful you are to love.'

He used to sing that to me when he dressed me to go out in the snow. I could smell his aftershave. He was like . . . He was like . . . He was like a mother to me sometimes."

"Was he?" says Blumenthal.

"He was all there was," I say. "He was the only game in town. He was a father to my brother. He let my brother be like him. He took my brother places; fishing. But he wouldn't let me—he wouldn't let me love him in the end. That was all I wanted, all I wanted to do, and he wouldn't let me." I have calmed down completely now. "He still won't," I say. I rub my eyes. "He still won't." I look at Blumenthal, finally. "When will it all be over?" I ask him. "When will these people stop running my life? Most people aren't tormented by their parents like this."

"Most people are insane. You're merely neurotic. Count yourself lucky."

"That's not true, you're just saying that. Most people are normal."

Blumenthal shrugs.

"I want to have a baby," I say.

"I'm sorry, but the Board of Regents would take my license."

"Not with you, Shrink. With my husband. What's-his-

name. John Kennedy. Superman. I love him so much. I
want to have his child."

"Have you discussed this with Clark?"

"Arthur—oh. No. Well, I mean, we've talked about it. We
both want kids . . ." I feel like I'm trying to pop the question. I pop it: "Do you think I can handle it?"

He gives this a fairly long think for him. Maybe twenty-
thirty seconds. Then, very carefully, he says, "Sometimes
people—all people, but I happen to see it in patients a
lot—want to have kids as a way of remaking themselves.
Which is great unless the kid has some silly notion of being
him or herself in all his teary, snotty glory. Then you get
what, in technical parlance, we call: a problem. I'll tell you
this much: kids play every string of you. No matter what
your child-rearing philosophy is, they'll be affected by
every part of you right down to your toes. You can't pro-
tect them from yourself. Other than that, I think I have to
let you and Supe make the decision."

I nod. More than anything else, I am trying to fight the
sinking, sick feeling I get in my stomach as I realize that
Blumenthal has children. That he is a father. He is a man.
He is a human being. "Do you know the way to San José?" I
ask.

"Pardon?"

"Nothing. Oh, Jesus!" I cover my eyes. "I can't stand it. I
can't stand any of it."

"Bear but a touch of my robe," says Blumenthal, "and
you shall be upheld in more than this."

"Oh," I say, laughing. "Oh, you *dirty* old man!"

I went to the march yesterday: U.S. out of Nicaragua.
No one had any clue we were going to invade, and so it was
amazing that such a huge number of people showed up.
Fifth Avenue was, as they say, a sea of humanity, heads,
banners, children on the shoulders of their fathers—a
ceaseless flow. The cameras on top of their vans peered
down at us with their single, black eyes and we raised two
fingers in the peace symbol for the folks back home. We
sang, "We shall overcome," and "Kumbaya." It made me

melancholy. I wanted to sing, "And did those feet, in ancient times, walk upon England's mountains green. . . ?" I mean, something radical, something new. It was all the sixties, a poor imitation of the sixties. I guess I went less because of the Nicaragua coup, than because of the Soviet troops massing in Germany. I wanted them to see that not all of us were for this. That some of us read Blake and were for Mental, not Corporeal, War. I can just see the Commissar or whatever with his ear glued to the TV speaker, saying, "Wait a minute, Comrade. Someone is singing the prologue to 'Milton.' Call back the bombs."

I missed the sixties—that is, I was a child when all the anti-war protests and drugs and long hair were going on. All that history—it was just TV to me, most of it was not even that. Sometimes, that makes me sad, like the men you meet who were too young for World War II and too old for Korea and spend the rest of their lives with a chip on their shoulders, hoping someone will shoot at them so they can prove themselves or searching for adventures "like war," or ashamed of their cowardice because they know, secretly, they *don't* want to get shot at because, I mean, really, who does? I guess it's just rare that we can indulge our love of violence—which, my theory goes, is just an attempt to repress our love of death by controlling the death of another—in a clearly justifiable way. It's what myths are made of. King Arthur, the wild west, World War II: the moment when the good guys could slaughter the bad guys, and be *right*. I don't know if I see the sixties like that, but it was a time, it seems to me, when people were willing to try something, to do something. It was an exciting time, and I wasn't there.

In retrospect, maybe the sixties were like son of World War II, a whole generation of men and women rebelling against their parents: the Fezziwig era, when we were engaged. Now, the slow roll into Scroogian anality and grasping: money has always been the symbol of this age, my age.

And so—will Marley come? Will Tiny Tim live? I see an empty stool by the fireplace, and a crutch carefully preserved. But are these the shadows of the things that must be, or the shadows of the things that *may* be? We are marching, heaven knows where we are marching. We'll know we're there.

People made speeches on a bandstand near the 42nd Street Library and the sound was broadcast through speakers hung on lampposts all the way up to the park. Some people were making real radical speeches—and bombing, pardon the pun. Their fists pounding the air, their faces turning red, their spit flying. "But *we* say—*out now!*" No applause. It was embarrassing. Others made special interest speeches: "We cannot end this threat to our earth until we solve the problems of the third world"; "colored people"; "women." My heart sank: something is wrong with this, and it may be too late to figure out what. The only optimistic note was that, every time a virgin walks by the library, one of the stone lions is supposed to roar— and I, for one, didn't hear a sound.

The problem with the sixties, I think, was that we— they—mistook philosophy for ability. They cried "Peace," they believed in peace, but there was still violence in their souls—maybe the very thing that made them cry and be- lieve in peace to begin with. Did they think they could escape their fantasies so easily? Do we think we can bury them now beneath a cache of gold? Any more than they could slay them with the Nazis, or outlaws, or dragons? Men's courses will foreshadow certain ends . . .

I left the march early. I rode up to my ritzy apartment, and watched the quiet avenue below and sipped tomato juice. I was humming to the Commissar:

"I will not cease from Mental Fight,
Nor shall my Sword sleep in my hand,
Till we have built Jerusalem
In England's green & pleasant Land."

I tried the radio, but there was nothing but news, and I already knew the news.

Lately, I think of Gordon, who was unkind. Poor Gor- don, half black, half white, all mean; clear, clear through. I

met him in a bar. In that year or so after Jerry, I guess I
met just about everyone in a bar. When I think about that
time, it seems to me it all took place in a vast silence: the
silence of my apartment in the Village, where I wrote the
elegant philosophical verse, stripped of all flesh, gleaming
like a polished skull. I remember Ted Hughes' "Crow": the
severed male head being smothered by the disembodied
vulva as God struggled to part them. My poetry then must
have sounded something like the silent struggle of
Hughes' God.

Mostly, I drank from a bottle in my room, so maybe, too,
I remember the silent amber of the scotch in the bottle. I
did go to bars—all the bars—and there was music there,
terribly loud music, and lights, but I remember it all in
shadowy silence.

I met Gordon—Gordon Waters—in a tavern named The
Stiff-Necked Giraffe, on the upper west side. I was drinking and guys were trying to pick me up, and I was doing
what I always did then—leading them on, flirting, kissing
them—then dumping them—saying bye with a finger to
their chins, and a flick of my backside. I'm still not sure
whether these were acts of anger or fear. Maybe both.

I could drink, though, I could hold my liquor, and so
could Gordon. He was standing—short, slim, broad-shoul-
dered, coffee-skinned, frizzy-haired—at the center of the
bar, talking to the bartender, and the people standing
around him were laughing. I edged closer, and ordered
another drink, and Gordon saw me out of the corner of his
eye, and began, I thought, to play to me. He was doing a
routine—a comedy routine—about the dirty words you
weren't allowed to say on the radio. Gordon was a disc
jockey at a jazz station, it turned out, but he wanted to be a
stand-up comic. I don't remember what he was saying—I
was too busy paying attention to the way I presented myself—but it was fairly funny in a vulgar way—"So I called
up the FCC, and we're on the air, I say, so, 'I forgot, man,
could you tell me just *which* words were restricted, man,'
and he says, 'Wuh-uh-wuh-uh—well, as you know, of
course—' he's a white dude—'as you know, of course, anything having to do with, uh, poo-poo is a no-no.' 'Poo-poo

no-no, gotcha, Jack.'" Well, everyone was laughing and I was drunk, and it seemed witty at the time.

I would like to say that later—after he bought me the drink—after he'd said, "Hey, pretty lady . . ." and that little signal had gone off in my brain saying "I can handle this guy," that lying signal that distinguishes between truth and bullshit as if bullshit were less likely to sweep you away just because you recognize it—I would like to say that I was not entranced by his job and the trappings of his job. After all, I'd been in publishing, was still in movies, I'd held glamour positions more or less. But there is something different about radio. Maybe it's the music. Deep down, in his heart of hearts, beyond his desire for immortality, for sexual completeness, for the peace of death, deep down, everyone really just wants to be a jazz singer. If, for one minute, I could stand on a stage and shout the words, "choinin' and a-boinin' funk!" into a microphone without someone shouting back, "Next!" I might well retire as from a job well done. Disc jockeys—they do something more recognizable, more approachable: they play the records: it is like standing in front of the mirror and mouthing the words; it is like masturbation: music from your fingertips.

When, alone in my room around midnight, I would lay down my pen and turn on the radio and hear Gordon nearly whisper, "And now, here's one for a very special little lady down in ye olde Greenwich Village," and when Ella Fitzgerald and Louis Armstrong would come on with "Moonlight in Vermont," I didn't say to myself "Moonlight in Vermont? What have Gordon and I got to do with Vermont?" I simply felt I was being sung to and was singing; like the world was an old musical and love was the sudden ability to sing.

I suppose I was in love again, although, at that time, it wasn't really to the point to wonder. Everything was muzzy and mellow and amber and silent—I was drunk, in other words—and I would say it to myself—"I'm in love," and I didn't wonder—I felt hollow, but I drank and I didn't wonder. It was all, really, panic in a cowl, because when Gordon would say, "Hey, baby, no strings," I would nod with my eyelids half closed, and twirl a strand of auburn around my fingers, and lift my glass and say, "That's right, man. Fuck all that." But if he was silent for more than ten seconds, I would say, "So whatcha thinking over there?" If he said, "I really dig you, baby," I would glow with it for hours, and then I would begin to ask myself, "That means love, doesn't it? Dig. To dig. Or, at least, 'like.' What does 'dig' mean, exactly?" and I would subside into amber silence and wait, desperate without knowing I was desperate, just muzzy and hollow, for him to say it or anything like it, again. And when we had sex, which was only about once a week, when he would spread the lips of my vagina with his fingers, and then stroke me a few times until I was wet (and me with my eyes closed, desperately conjuring what was now a shadowy figure in a mask—but with suspiciously long hair and rounded figure—approaching with the brand—oh, the repressed is like a bola, wrapping itself around your throat tighter and tighter and tighter and tighter), when he would slip his small erection inside of me, bury his face in my hair, and pump for a minute and a half and squirt and roll over and say, "Hey, baby, that was fine," I wanted, when it was over, to have clutched his buttocks to me, to have closed my legs and captured him inside me, to have never let him go. I began to forget to use my diaphragm now and then. And I stopped using it altogether after that night at the Komedy Klub. Oh, what a krummy night that was.

Gordon had been practising his routines on me for weeks—a terrible thing to do to someone. You sit there alone with him in your apartment, straddling a chair, clutching a drink, while he stands before you as if you were an entire audience and tells you jokes. I didn't even hear half of them, the pain at the corner of my lips was so great from smiling. What was I supposed to do? Say, "Not funny, Gordon"? I knew what that felt like from my parents and, anyway, the few times I suggested changes, he would say, "That? No, that's *funny*, girl," and then he would drop it from the routine without further discussion.

So, finally, we went to the Komedy Klub, one of those bars on the east side where they let comedians debut. It was summer, and the place was filled with college students, which was good because they're hip and out for a good time. Gordon was on sometime after eleven, but was held up for about ten minutes when Tom Safire—who was then starring in that TV show about black men dressing up as white women dressing up as black men—breezed in unexpectedly. The audience went wild with applause and laughter and he did some of his manic routines. I fully expect Gordon's bad end to include the murder of that man. He never forgave him. "It's whores like that Safire, they keep the people, I mean, the *real* people, they keep them *down*, that Safire." I go to all his films.

No haze of liquor could have dulled the next three minutes of that night. When Gordon took the stage, with all the moves, the gestures, the words he had learned from the comics on TV—"Thank you. Thank you very much, ladies and gentlemen"—I felt my entire body close on my stomach like a mousetrap.

"Thank you. I want to thank that warm-up guy, he could go far," referring to Safire, and the audience gave him a little ripple of laughter, that ripple that sounds like "Show me," like the great Not Funny gavel is suspended in the air above the judge's bench. "Now, Tom is lucky, he's *all* black. I'm only half black, see. That's a problem. If I get too close to a pistol, man, my left arm grabs it, points it at the right side of my head, and shouts, 'Stick 'em up, honky!'"

Oh, oh, oh, I was so glad I was a poet then. What soaring metaphors you can construct even while puking and shitting off a hangover; what Ariel might spring forth from what crippled Pope; what moments of brilliance even in poverty and rejection. But if you are a performer, God help you, your outer body is the vessel of the gift: you are out there in the flesh. The difference between being panned as a writer and as a performer is the difference between being insulted and being hit in the face with a chair. When they crucify a performer, the nails go into his soul, yes, but they get there by way of his hands; when they drop the plastic bag of silence, they drop it, not on his reputation, his insecurity, his anger—they drop it over his head so he can't breathe. And there is no silence on earth like the absence of laughter.

I heard Gordon's breath, a half laugh at his own joke, magnified by the microphone into a black desert wind. Three more minutes. Three more minutes without a sound but the sound of his voice. I laughed, of course, or tried, but now even I could see that the jokes I had giggled at in my apartment were either empty or filled with all the wrong things, either wholly unoriginal ("All comedians borrow material," he had told me.) or so angry that even the cruelest members of the audience looked down into their drinks. No big yuks are going to come out of a joke—it occurred to me too late—that begins, "My fucking parents really screwed me up, man . . ." By the time it was over—and Gordon persevered nobly to the end, I'll give him that—Gordon had tears in his eyes, and his voice sounded like a shovel scraping out the grave of every line, and all his ambitions.

I had to go outside afterwards so he wouldn't see me crying. I slipped away through the polite applause, and by the time he reached me in the back, I was red-eyed but composed: the best I could do.

We rode back to my place in silence, and I made drinks, although I was already nauseous and my head was swimming.

"I'll tell you what it is," said Gordon. He was standing in the center of the room with his head bowed, and his eyes glaring at the worn carpet: he looked like a vulture. "I'll tell you what it is, it's that fucking Tom Safire. I mean, that place is for new talent, he had no right coming in there like that. Because, you see, that was not right. I mean, fucking Safire, he just fucked me, that's all, that's what he did, right there."

I couldn't help it: I did the worst possible thing: I started to cry.

Gordon looked up. "What—what you crying for, girl. Oh, you gonna pity me? You gonna feel good about yourself because you can say 'Poor Gordon'?"

I shook my head desperately, my hair flying back and forth across my face, but I couldn't speak.

Gordon grabbed me by the shoulders and began to shake me. "Stop crying," he shouted.

"Don't!" I cried, and I got the hiccoughs.

He tossed me aside, and I caught my breath. The crying eased: he had shaken it out of me.

Gordon sat down on the edge of the bed and put his face in his hands. "Fucking Saphire," he said.

I went to him and put my hand on his shoulder. He shrugged it off. He raised his head and sat with his hands on his knees, glowering at the middle distance. I probably should have left him alone—I admit that much—but I did not want to be excluded from his misery. I knelt on the floor next to him.

"Let me," I whispered, and reached to unzip his fly.

He grabbed a handful of my hair and I gasped as he yanked my head back.

"What are you, a fucking pro?" he said.

"Gordon, you're hurting me." What a stupid thing to say: why else would he pull my hair?

"Don't come at me with your filth, woman. You're worse than that fucking Safire."

Then, very deliberately, with a sort of calm, grim purpose, he put his fist in my eye and began to grind it against my flesh.

"Gordon!" I screamed, and he flung me to the floor, where I lay clutching my streaming eye and moaning.

Gordon got up. "I'm getting out of here," he said.

And I heard myself shriek, "No! Wait!" even as a low hum started to repeat over and over in the back of my mind, "I'm drunk, I'm just very, very drunk, I'm really, really, I'm just really drunk," and I started to pull myself to him across the floor on my knees, saying, "I'm sorry. I didn't mean anything. Don't go. I'm sorry," and thinking, "I'm drunk, I'm very drunk, that's all. I'm just really, really drunk."

I didn't even pretend that night that the diaphragm was forgotten. Its absence was some compensation for the way he ploughed into me, for the pain. It was as if the possibility of getting pregnant somehow balanced the humiliation of being treated like that—and of begging to be treated like that. It was a night, that is to say, of pure Komedy all around.

Gordon went home in the dark, as usual, and the next morning, I went out and took a walk around Washington Square. It was a fairly balmy summer's day and all the street painters were out displaying their aqua seascapes, and their detailed skylines, and their bright circus scenes and it was very colorful and European and melancholy and nice. As I was walking past one of them—a portrait painter in a blue smock with a black beret on her long brown hair—she called from her stool, "Portrait painted?" I stopped and turned to her and she saw my black eye. "Oops," she said. I just stood there, kind of contemplating her. She had a kind face.

At first, she turned away but when I didn't move—I was kind of at gaze, I guess—she looked up again, squinting against the sun, and said, "A boy do that?"

I nodded.

"I could leave it out of the picture."

"How much?"

"Five bucks," she said.

"Leave it in," I told her, and sat down on the subject's stool.

So Elizabeth painted a portrait of me with a black eye— I've lost it since: I could never hang it up with Gordon around, and by the time he left, I couldn't remember where I put it—and we talked. We didn't talk about Gordon. Mostly, Elizabeth talked about Kansas, and her parents—whom she always referred to as Buck and Allie— and how she was about to graduate from Cooper Union, and had landed a job designing sets for a little theater off-off-Broadway, but would probably have to teach also, and she had a friend at the School of Visual Arts and so on. What she did, I guess, was just give me a break from it, let me sit and dream my way into her serene life, the quiet waters of her soul. Elizabeth has that effect on people. Her portrait showed me gazing off wistfully through the purple bruise.

Afterward, we went to the Black Coffee and had coffee together—which seems, now I think of it, to be the constant of our friendship. And then, we picked up a loaf of french bread at Hitler's, and a bottle of white wine and went back to Elizabeth's where she made us fondue.

By then, we were talking nonstop, laughing nonstop. I had told her about my parents, and Jerry, and she had listened in that quiet, intense way she has. We were—I was thinking even then—like Jack Kerouac and Dean Moriarty in the back of the car, discovering the IT in conversation. We had connected, and the stories of our lives flowed from our mouths into each other and twined together seamlessly.

Gordon never liked Elizabeth. He always got very superior and domineering when she was around. He would pontificate on the effect of the media on such-and-such or, worse, the state of comedy in America today. He used the word—the three words—"Re-al-ity" a lot, and sometimes he stood next to me with his hand on the top of my head like the statue of Daniel Webster in Central Park with his hand on the book on the lectern. But he never attacked Elizabeth directly. He was snide behind her back enough, but I think, frankly, he was afraid of her. And as for Elizabeth, she avoided him as much as she could and we mostly met at her place, where I would sometimes lie on the couch and read my movie scripts while she worked on her set designs, and sometimes vomit into her toilet and pass out on her bathroom floor while she stroked my hair silently and my heart bled and thrilled at the aloofness, the sternness in her eyes.

But if Gordon didn't like Elizabeth, he hated Lansky, whom Elizabeth met at the theater. I think he hated Lansky as much as he hated Tom Safire, and I even seem to remember him mentioning them both in one sentence. I was sitting in the chair by the window reading Lansky's latest and chuckling, and he said something like, "Don't laugh at that garbage, baby. That's not funny. Lansky? That's like, I mean, it's like Safire."

Lansky, to be fair, treated Gordon like he wasn't there, and I remember once, when Gordon met me at a rehearsal of "Dying Embers," Gordon said, "Wouldn't it be funnier if Angela threw the drink in his face?" and Lansky thought

about it and just said, "No," and walked away, which just
about turned the sod over the mound with the headstone
marked Lansky-Safire.

But, in truth, I think the thing that bothered Gordon
most was Lansky's jokes about my drinking. Lansky is
almost a spartan about things like this. He gets drunk, I'd
say, just about once every time there's a serious threat of
nuclear holocaust. Lansky also differs from Elizabeth in
that, while he, too, conceives deep, lasting and loyal affec-
tions for people, for some reason, no doubt involving his
personal history, he has no vocabulary for them, so that, in
Lansky's mouth, an expression of concern over my drinking habits would come out, "Good, Sam, have another one,
there's still a healthy spot in your liver." This would absolutely infuriate Gordon who would say something sweet
like, "Hey, just lay off, man, okay?" thus bringing whatever
gathering was in progress to an abrupt and embarrassed
conclusion. At the time, this sort of turned me on—I clung
to these moments as expressions of Gordon's protec-
tiveness of me, his caring. But, of course, they weren't that.
They weren't that, at all.

Anyway, I think it was all these new friends I was making—that and the slow dawning of the realization that he
would never have the courage to go on stage again—that
finally made Gordon do what he did. Which was cheat on
me, which, in my guise as tough-hard-drinking-gal, I was
not supposed to mind that much—Hey, no strings,
right?—and which he therefore rubbed in my face like so
much ground glass.

Gordon came by less often, and a couple of times, he let
me get the whiff of her perfume; let me see her lipstick on
his handkerchief, or he'd tell me some long story about "a
friend" and "she was saying to me . . ." These were always
the days when we would have sex, as if my knowledge of
the infidelity coursed through his cock like blood, and he
would say, "How do you like it, baby?" in the few seconds
before he would come into my open womb, and I would
say, "Oh, oh, oh," as if I were coming, too.

One day, he had coffee with her in the Black Coffee—a
tall, cool, beautiful, very-black woman with a lean, pointed

face, like a cat's (well, it was). He knew—and I knew he knew—I was coming in there with Elizabeth that day and I saw him spot me from the corner of his eye before he delved back, ever-so-deeply, into their no doubt scintillating conversation. They weren't holding hands or necking or anything. I couldn't have confronted them, accused them. I couldn't have, anyway; there were no strings, no strings, and the voice in my head, almost ceaseless now—"I am so drunk, I am really drunk"—had developed a sort of silent counterpoint that it at once harmonized with and obscured: "If I lose him, I will become horrible; nothing; I will die." Elizabeth took me by the elbow and guided me out the door. We went to another restaurant, but she wouldn't talk to me about it—she had only told me once to leave him and I had slugged back a scotch and told her she was such a prig. Now, when I began drinking heavily, she paid her tab and left me alone.

That was the month, finally. It was in the bleak December, it was, it was, when I finally missed my period. I have never had heavy periods, and they've always been fairly regular, and so I've never really been one of these Oh-God-I'm-on-the-rag girls—although, come to think of it, I can see why I would have liked then to ignore the whole thing. But with Gordon, every month had become a little abortion, a castration even, a little death, a never-to-be-a-baby dribbling down my thighs; a loss of the only power I felt I had over him, to keep him—and I had to keep him because, oh God, I was just so drunk.

Well, I was due around December first, and by December ninth, I was sure. It was a crisp, clear night and I was thinking of the country, where we would live and there would be sparkling stars.

I sat and drank, slowly but steadily, and listened to him on the radio. I remember he played Hubert Laws' "Afro Classic"—"Fire and Rain"—and how I thought it was the best piece of jazz music I had ever heard, and how, near the end of it, I suddenly realized somehow that he was playing it for her, and I closed my legs together tightly and shivered—I was so drunk——as I sipped my scotch. At least, I thought, at least, she isn't from Vermont, either.

And I heard him say, as from a distance—as across a distance of rippling amber silence—"And so, this is Gordon Waters, wishing you a very pleasant—" Pause—I knew that pause to the second and he and I spoke together: "Goodnight."

Then maybe I dozed a little, because I remember him coming in, suddenly, as if there had been a bad cut in a piece of film, and he was saying, "*Good* show tonight. *Good* show. Make me a drink, will you, baby."

So I did, and I sat down again heavily with the scotch bottle, and I was thinking, "God, I'm drunk," and I said, "Gordon, I think I'm pregnant."

He looked at me a moment with what I believe is called a frozen smile, and then he just started to shake his head, great big shakes, and wave his hand before me as if to ward me off and he said, "Oh no. Oh no. Absolutely not, baby. That is too heavy for me, girl. That is just too heavy. No. Huh uh."

I have often wished that I had asked him what exactly he meant by that. Was that "No, you're not pregnant," or "No, you may not say you are pregnant," or "No, you *have* not said it, are not here at all"? But I did not ask him that. Instead, I said in a small voice: "Should I have an abortion?"

But this received another negative as Gordon said: "I don't . . . You just deal with it. You just *deal* with it, baby, cause this is *way* too heavy for *me.* Huh uh."

Would he have made the same answer (I think he would) if I had said, "But, Gordon, I'm dying," or "But, Gordon, I'm dead," in the same way I now whined, "But, Gordon, I'm *pregnant.*"

"No way, baby. No way," said Gordon.

My lip began to tremble. "I am so drunk," I thought. I said: "Well, okay, if you want me to, I'll get it fixed."

And he exploded. His face contorted, pressed close to mine, his arms surrounding me as his hands grabbed the arms of my chair so fiercely I thought he would fling both me and it out the window, he screamed: "What are you trying to do? What are you trying to do with this bullshit? You trying to fix me?" I turned from him, afraid he would

punch me and he grabbed my face in one hand, squeezing
it in his hand and screaming, "You want to fix it good,
don'tcha, so I can't *be* what I wanna *be*. You wanna make
me nothing. That's all: nothing. That's all you *ever* want!"
He flung my head back against the chair. "Well, how would
you like it—how would you like some of *this?*"

He dashed across the room to my writing desk by the
window. He yanked open the drawer so hard that the
flower vase on the desk fell over, the water coughing out,
the daisies drooping. Screaming, "How about some of
*this?*" he ripped my notebook out of the drawer.

I stood up and smashed the scotch bottle on the edge of
the lampstand. The crash, the glass, the spraying liquor
terrified me, and my hands shook as I pointed the bottle at
him and screamed, "Put it back!"

"What are you, fucking crazy?"

"Put it, put it, Gordon, put it!"

"Put down that bottle, girl."

"Put it or I'll kill you, Gordon," I said, and I was sober as
a judge.

He put it down. He hesitated for a moment, but then he
smirked and snorted and he dropped it back into the
drawer. I couldn't move. I stood there trembling, clutching the broken bottle in both hands, pointing it at him.

Gordon shot his cuffs. "You're crazy, baby," he said.
"This is over for me. This is over for this boy right here."
He started swaggering toward the door.

"Don't leave me," I whispered, starting to cry, following
him, as he walked, with the jagged edge of the bottle.

"You're crazy, girl, you need help," he said.

"Please, oh please, don't, don't go," I said, pointing the
bottle at him.

"You're fucking out of your mind," said Gordon—and
that's how it ended: with me pointing that broken bottle at
the slamming door, and begging him not to go.

Or not quite. That is, I suppose, it really ended when,
after the door shut, I fell back into the chair, moaning,
beyond tears, just moaning like a creature in pain, and
then suddenly doubled over, clutching my stomach, with
the worst cramp I have ever had, and then, relaxing,

became aware of the dampness that had gathered in my underwear, and so knew that my period had begun.

Elizabeth, I guess, was angry at me over the scene in the Black Coffee because she didn't come to see me for over a month. Most of that time I spent drunk. One night I spent with a man named Hank, a married executive-type who had sex with me, I think, after I'd taken him back to my apartment and passed out.

When Elizabeth finally did come by, I guess she could see that I wasn't in the best of shape, but she held her tongue because I told her that Gordon was gone and I guess she thanked heaven for small blessings. She made us coffee, of course, and stayed to chat for a long time. But all through the conversation, I kept feeling myself floating away from her, away from her and everything as if the world were a dock and I had not been properly secured. I wanted to call out, to call to Elizabeth to bring me back in, but I knew if she did, if I got too close, she would see me for the horror, the monstrosity I really was; she would see that I was not fit for humankind and push me off again, this time forever.

When she finally left—she had stayed much longer than she'd meant to, and she had to meet Lansky for dinner, and when she finally left, I sat on the edge of the bed with my hands dangling between my knees, just staring at the portfolio case she had accidentally left behind. I'm sure I must have stared at it for hours.

I was in love with my therapist and yet aware that I must one day lose him to my own redemption; I was haunted by not-funny memories of not-funny Gordon, and less-funny thought of deadpanned Dad; the U.S. had overturned the government of Nicaragua and the Russians, let me tell you, were miffed; I wanted to have my beloved husband's baby and was worrying at my motives like the proverbial dog avec proverbial bone—and this was the week God decided to crack open like one not-very-cosmic egg and lay his woes upon my elegantly shaped head. Which only goes to prove the old saying I just made up that trying to live as if tranquility were the status quo is like treating the surf as a lake disturbed by occasional waves. It's the surfboard we want, my darlings: the method.

So—God. He called me down there in the cluttered, white cubicle in the basement of St. Sebastian's and it was, as they say, intense from the very start. I answered the phone to find only the sound of weeping, and when I asked who was there, received a piteous, terrified wail for answer:

"This—is—G-a-a-a-ad!"

"What?" I said. "What's—what? What's the matter?"

"Oh, something. Oh, something awful is going to happen. Oh, if only I hadn't loved you, Sam. If only I *didn't* love you."

Calmly dropping my jaw to my chest, I suavely slapped my reddening cheek with one hand and dropped back in my chair with a poise that I must say was commendable. I realized then the shock, the shock and the control, that must have lain behind that one grave Blumenthalian nod when I told him of my love for him. He must be used to it by now, but then—maybe it is always a shock to be loved—or maybe it was just me, just the shock of the similarity between what I had said to Blumenthal and what God was saying to me. I had neither the time nor the courage to face, for the moment, the psychic implications of being thrust, for this particular nonce, into Blumie's shoes, and so I contented myself as I began to recover, with wondering whether, out of this chain of secrets, of dark terrors, forged between God and me and Blumenthal, and maybe his therapist and maybe his therapist's wife and maybe his therapist's wife's mother and maybe his therapist's wife's mother's priest and so, possibly, back to God—whether out of this chain we might yet forge another chain, a better one.

I used an old jogger's trick—taught to me, of course, by an old jogger—which is to control your breath and speak clearly so the fellow ahead of you won't know how winded you really are.

"Do you think that it's wrong to love me, God?" I asked.

"Something terrible will happen, and I shouldn't have done it, but I didn't know, I didn't know . . ."

"Didn't know . . .?"

"That it was wrong, that something so terrible would happen if she found me."

"Your mother."

He only sobbed.

"Because she found you loving someone?"

He croaked on an intake of breath: "Yes."

"A girl? A boy?"

"Myself!" he wailed.

"She found you masturbating, and she punished you."

Another choked: "Yes."

"How? How did she punish you, God?"

He started shrieking at me, and I felt his hysteria run into me and become, in part, my own. "I can't! I can't! I can't! I can't! I can't!"

What's funny—not hilarious funny, but odd funny—is how minor, really, another person's secrets seem for the most part. I never did find out how God's mother punished him, but I did assume a terrible abuse—and God knows that parents are capable of it with that little helpless ball of not-themselves in their power and yet out of their control. Yet even if it was as bad as I could imagine—and I have, I suppose, quite an imagination—it somehow did not seem commensurate with what became of him. Human childhood, I am convinced, by nature creates neurosis, the neurosis of life dying to its infinite possibilities. There is no way—this, I think, is what Blumenthal was trying to tell me—no way to raise an enlightened child, even if you raise a relatively well-adjusted one like Arthur. But can this dreadful place, this earth, these babies starving under Arthur's eyes in Africa, these Judy Honeggers blown to kingdom come, these missiles stationed nose to nose, these gas chambers, these empires, this history, be nothing more than an immense construct atop the little moment when a child's fingers are yanked away from his own flesh? It does not seem possible that so great and terrible a cathedral could be built on the head of a pin but, on the other hand, once it has been accomplished, once you have prayed in the cathedral, have worked there, once you have been

married in it and had children and had children die there
and slid your parents into its vaults, once you have waged
war for control of the cathedral, debated the best course
for the cathedral's future, written a thousand articles for
the cathedral's newspaper—how, then, do you begin to
pull the pin free?

"God," I said, into his sobbing.

"I love you, Sam, that's all: I just love you."

"Tell me what she did to you," I said.

"I can't."

"Why?"

"Because you couldn't bear it."

"But I will."

He paused, catching his breath. I waited, having already
lost mine.

"I think I have to go now," he said.

"God . . ."

"I think—I'm sorry—I think I have to go. I'm sorry."

And I was silent. I sat there, feeling myself losing him,
and simply couldn't think of anything to say.

"I love you, Sam," he said again.

And then I thought of something. "I love you, too,
God," I said—happy, especially considering Dr. B. and me,
to discover that it was the truth.

"I have to—I have to do it," he said—and he hung up.

Well, I wandered about, and I wandered about and I
wandered about some more in the summer evening. And
as I finally headed up Fifth Avenue for home, the sky was
hanging onto the daylight by its fingernails, as it will in
early July, and the air was riffling the sodden heat with a
breeze from the East River.

I came into the apartment to find Arthur lying on the
couch, reading some court papers and wearing a Mickey
Mouse hat. He glanced up and said, "Ah!" and continued
reading.

I sat down on the edge of the couch, my shoulders
hunched, head hung, staring at the floor. Then I took a
peek at the hub.

"Nice hat," I told him.

He tried to look up at it. "It's for you. I got it for you for your birthday."

I squeezed his thigh. "That was nice of you. My birthday's in April."

"I couldn't remember, so I panicked: I thought—if I don't know when it is it might be today."

I laughed, then I sighed. I climbed over him and lay down on the couch with my head on the opposite arm, facing him, and my legs surrounding him as his stockinged feet pressed against my vagina, making me hum.

He stripped the hat off and handed it to me and I put it on.

"You look depressed," he said.

"I'm supposed to look like Mickey Mouse."

"You look like Mickey Mouse when he gets depressed."

"Easy with the big toe," I said.

Arthur set his papers on the floor. "How about a little tender loving cunnilingus?" he said.

"Oh, you lawyers with your forked tongues."

But he didn't move—which was pure Arthur: always the appropriate thing. In this case, to wait.

I had my head leaned back on the arm, and was staring at the ceiling, warming to his toes. But now I took his foot in my hand and felt it waggling.

"MacArthur?" I said.

"MacMa'am?"

"Did your mother ever—catch you—doing something?"

"Never, but Frenchie and the forger bought it on the Rhine."

"Seriously."

"Okay. You mean, I take it, something of the sexual persuasion."

"I do."

"Yes, as a matter of fact," said Arthur. "She walked in on me once when I was playing doctor with Claire Rutherford."

"Not the infamous Claire Rutherford?"

"Terror of Europe, the very one."

"How old were you?"

"Six, seven, eight, I don't know."

"You don't remember?"

"Seven."

"What did she say?"

" 'Oh, Doctor, Doctor!' "

"I mean your mother, bobo."

"Oh." Arthur considers. His toes wiggle pleasantly against my fingers. "I don't rightly recall," he says. "Something about 'that nice Schweitzer boy.' "

"No."

"No. I don't know. I think she asked us if we wanted milk and cookies, and we did."

"She broke it up."

"What was she going to do?"

"Don't get defensive," I say.

He doesn't answer me and I am glad because it was a creepy thing to say.

"Were you embarrassed?" I asked him.

"Tolerably. All those naked chocolate chips blossoming wantonly beside the creamy white milk . . ."

"All right, all right."

"Yes. I was embarrassed, and Claire was mor-ti-fied. But we'd been pretty quick about covering up and, anyway, to be quite frank, it was bloody well worth it."

"Did your father have a chat with you?"

"Yes." Arthur laughs fondly; my lucky Arthur. "He waited just long enough so I was supposed to not think it was connected to the event, if you get my drift."

"Nice try, Dad."

"Yeah."

"What did he say?"

"Oh, the usual in his own inimitable fashion. 'Dashed fine thing, this sex business, dashed fine, what?' "

"But . . .?"

"But—we gentlemen must be considerate, sensitive, steadfast, loyal, true—and try to remember that every cunt has a human being attached to it."

"Chester didn't say that."

"Chester didn't say that."

Taking off the mouse ears and tossing them to the floor, I lift my head to look at him. He is watching me quietly, hands folded on his abdomen. He is smiling wryly, and yet not warily, not cautiously. He is simply watching me, waiting.

"Have you slept with a lot of different women?"

"You're the seventeenth." Pure Arthur.

"Were any of them as good as me?"

"Not one."

"Arthur."

"All of them."

"Arthur!"

"Some of them."

"*Arthur!*"

"I pass. Try History for 80, Art."

"Arthur, do you think people have souls?"

"Well," says Arthur, considering. "I deal with lawyers all day, but I suppose it's possible. What do you mean, exactly?"

"Well, I mean, do you think it's possible that, say, two twins could have exactly the same upbringing and yet be entirely different?"

"Oh—you mean, like, do they have some ground level—essence to begin with?"

"Yeah."

"Yeah, I suppose. Theoretically."

"I suppose," I say, "since you can't have a soul without a body, and can't have a body without a unique personal history, you can't have a soul without a unique personal history and the question becomes meaningless."

"That was my next guess," says Arthur, snapping his fingers.

I sigh. He watches. He smiles. He waits.

"Arthur," I say, "I want to have a baby."

"Really? Is Blumenthal allowed to do that?"

"Not with Blumenthal!" I wail. "With youmenthal."

"With mementhal?"

"I'm serious."

"Yes, well, it would be rough if we had to tell the poor tot we were just kidding, wouldn't it?"

I pinch his toes. He says ouch.

"Do you think I'd be a good mother?" I ask.

"Great."

"Arthur."

"Awful."

"Arthur!"

"Great-awful."

"The York-Lancaster conflict."

"What was the War of the Roses?"

Now, it is my turn. I smile at him. I wait. Finally, Arthur pulls his feet free, and sits up on the edge of the couch. He stares at the coffee table for a long moment, a-think. Then he looks up at me.

"Tell you what, Sam," he says. "Let's not."

"Not . . .?"

"Let's not have a baby."

"Ever?"

"No—right now." He stands up and starts to unbutton his shirt—he has already taken off his tie. "Let's not have a baby right this minute."

I consider, then sit up and begin undoing my blouse. "Do you think we shouldn't?"

"Absolutely."

My breasts are free. He is stepping out of his pants.

"How don't we do it?" I ask.

"We just—" Visionary in his jockey shorts, he raises his hands before him and gazes dreamily over my head. "—we make love to each other with every pore. We make love to our lost selves through each other. We let our penis and vagina expand over every inch of us until it doesn't matter which part of us is where or even if it's my part or your part, and if we finally do release, it will be all of us, both of us, blown away into forever for no earthly reason but the fun of it!"

"Why, Arthur!" I say, pulling my jeans and panties off just as fast as I can. I jump to my feet. We stand before each other, naked—naked, and totally at a loss.

"How do we start?" I ask him.

"How's this?" he says, and he sticks his elbow in my ear.

I fall to the couch laughing, and he is on top of me laughing, kissing me and laughing, kissing me everywhere and laughing and laughing and already with thee, Arthur: Tender is the night!

# Eight

This is what happened to me on Friday, the thirteenth of July: the day most people remember as the day the leaders of the great nations first exchanged threats of holocaust.

For me, it was, to begin with, the day Elizabeth and Lansky were married in a brief ceremony at eight a.m. at the U.N. chapel with both a minister and a rabbi presiding. Buck and Allie were there, looking, respectively, ovoid and shapeless, but smiling nonetheless and saying, "Yep, our little girl," a lot. Lansky's parents were there, too. They sat in the back pew because they didn't want to be any trouble. She was a very big woman who sat erect with her hands folded in her lap, trying to look like everything on earth was going exactly the way she had planned and arranged it, though it seemed to these hyper-sensitive eyes that she was unhappy about the whole thing: angry and afraid. Lansky's father, a series of sagging eggs placed one on top of another, wore a black suit, a wrinkled nose and a strained smile: he looked, throughout, as if he had just bent over to smell a rose and found a piece of shit in the middle of it.

Arthur was on don't-worry-Lansky detail, and I was saying fine-perfect-it's-beautiful-Elizabeth over and over and over again. She really was beautiful, too, in a knee-length, pink linen dress, and a lace posy in her hair. She was smiling so much that, at first, I thought she was just pretending to be happy. But she really was happy—she was just pretending not to be scared.

No one gave them away or anything, and there was no

143

best man or maid of honor per se. Arthur and I were the witnesses and stood behind and to one side of the couple while they were joined by the two clergymen Lansk called "the reb and preacher show." Lansky shook with terror and Elizabeth was as radiant as the sun and the only reportable highlight was when the rabbi asked Lansky if he planned to love and respect Elizabeth through sickness, health, wealth, poverty and the rest till death did they part and he said, "Do . . .? You're asking me? Yes. Absolutely. That's right."

"I do, Lansky," Elizabeth whispered.

"So do I," he said. "Absolutely."

Which apparently satisfied heaven and the state of New York and they were hitched. See Buck and Allie's snapshots for details.

Then, Arthur had to run to a bunch of meetings, and Buck and Allie went out to have a gander at the big city, and Mr. and Mrs. Lansky (the elder) went out to have breakfast which, Mrs. Lansky gave us to know, should have been provided for, and Reb and Preacher, I guess, headed to Atlantic City to play the dinner shows.

I walked outside with the new Mr. and Mrs. L., and we waited on the sidewalk in the morning sun for their cab to arrive. They were bound for the airport and thence Switzerland, which had triumphed over Lansky's Australia where he thought the fallout would come last.

Lansky (Mr.) glanced at his watch. They only had five hours to make the airport, which is twenty minutes away. Elizabeth had traded breakfast for Australia.

"Listen," I said, "I'm going to miss you guys."

"You won't have to if that cab doesn't show," said Mr.

"Don't worry, darling," said Mrs.

My eyes filled with tears. "I better go," I said.

Lansky came over and took me by the shoulders. "Listen," he said, "if we don't all meet again . . ."

"Sweetheart!" said Elizabeth.

"Well," said Lansky, "things are like that." And they were. "I just want you to know, Sam, that you're the closest potential cloud of radioactive vapor we have, and if you survive to write my biography, remember—I was the one who said we should have gone to Australia."

I threw my arms around his neck and kissed his cheek. "Go safely, Lansky, and come back soon," I said.

"Vaya con dios, Cutes," he said, and I released him and he turned away from me before his own tears could overflow and he walked to the corner to watch for the cab, and to leave Elizabeth and me alone.

Elizabeth took my hand and smiled.

"All well?" she asked.

"All well."

"We have a date for dinner and married-lady gossip in two weeks, right?"

"Two weeks," I said.

"So stop crying."

"Right. You, too."

"Right."

"You saved my life," I said.

And she gave me a classic Lansky shrug. "It was a slow day."

The cab arrived and Lansky Mr. hailed it with all kinds of fantastic gestures while simultaneously running back for the luggage and screaming for Lansky Mrs. to hurry up.

"Well," I said to her, "if this is the age of anxiety, I think you just married into royalty."

I threw myself into her arms and we embraced for a second of dying clarity.

"Oh God," I said, "can you bear how much I need you?"

"Yes," said Elizabeth.

I let her go. The Lanskys got in their cab, and while Mr. checked to see if his traveller's cheques were still in his shoe, Mrs. leaned out the window and waved to me.

"Send us a postcard from Nirvana, Sam," she called, and the taxi pulled away into the traffic, and then turned the corner and was out of sight.

So now, I am all alone. It is about eleven in the morning, I am too depressed to work, and Arthur will not even be in his office till after lunch so I can't call him to chat, and there's no earthly chance I'm going to start reading the newspaper, so I decide to walk up to the fifties and over to Third and see if there is an early movie showing.

I am in luck. By the time I get up there, the first showing of "The Twelve of Us," starring Tom Safire, one of my favorites, is about to begin. The Friday noon movie in New York is what I call the poet's screening, as the audience generally consists of five lean, bearded young men and two scrawny blonde women with close-cropped hair, all of them telling themselves, as the lights fade, that indolence is part of the art form, while three executives who are supposed to be at working lunches sidle to their seats in the deepening dark. At any rate, there's no line for tickets, and I walk up to the booth and the woman says, "How many?" though I'm standing there by myself, and I hear myself say to her:

"The great beast dies."

And as the woman stares at me as if I had said nothing—because I have not said "one" or "two" or "when's the next showing?" the only sounds of which her cockleshell ears can make sense, I think: Oh shit, a poem.

This is the last thing I want. That is, what I want is to go to the movies. I assure myself that it is merely the tip of the thing surfacing and that it will be days, maybe weeks, before the rest clears—and, for some not very subtle reasons, I think of the fact that my mother damn near gave birth to me in the cab because she refused to believe she was really in labor and, determined, I say:

"One, please," and reach for my purse as the ticket sticks out of the slot like a clown's tongue, and I think: The great beast dies, and vestal whores . . .

"Thank you," I say, taking the ticket—their breasts are bared and they are reaching upward, I can see them.

"Wanna pay?" says the woman in the glass cage.

I am flustered. "Oh, of course," I say, and put the ticket back on the counter as a sign of honesty and good will and return my attention to my purse and snap it open and think: The great beast dies and vestal whores, their bare breasts lifted to the holocaust skies, raise up their arms . . .

It is coming, as my mother herself might have said, too fast, and I already begin to fear that my mind will not be able to reach the end, tethered, by the fear of forgetting, to the beginning, and I give the ticket lady a smile and say, "Shit. Excuse me," and turn to walk briskly out onto the sidewalk.

The great beast dies,
And vestal whores, their bare breasts lifted
To the holocaust skies
Extend their arms . . .

And that's it. With the pressure of decision off me, the thing stops cold. I know if I can jot these lines down, it will either continue or announce itself finished for now—but am I carrying a pen? You jest, my Lord. Can I buy a pen in the middle of Manhattan? Not unless I can find a blind man fast. There is, however, a tobacco nook on this block and dangling from the cash register on a tired string is the pencil for marking lottery tickets and a man—father of five, beats his wife, is frittering away the rent—is painstakingly carving the number of pages in Rousseau's *Confessions* next to the number of movements in Haffner's Serenade or whatever when I mutter my apologies and snatch it from him for a moment in order to scrawl what I've got on the little piece of cardboard in my Kleenex pack.

I get as far as "The great beast dies," when the gambler finally manages to blink and say "Hey!" at the same moment—but that's okay, writing this down is enough to let me know: it's coming, all of it, and I've got to get home.

I hail a cab and collapse into the back with a sigh of relief: cabbies always carry pencils to keep their trip sheets with, and I am safe till we get home. Again, with the pressure lifted, the first lines of the poem just sort of float there on the surface of my mind like the first risen timber of a sunken ship. We sputter through the thick lunch hour traffic until we get to Park and then we breeze uptown.

I have been holding back, but as we turn onto 81st Street, I let myself go and am paying the man as I get—

always going back to the beginning to make sure I haven't left anything behind:

The great beast dies
And vestal whores, their bare breasts lifted
To the holocaust skies,
Extend their arms
For the fragments of his body's empire,
Falling and falling.

I am in the tortured throes of the realization that I am going to have to move the period back to empire and use falling and falling as the transition into my next thought or be caught in the prologue forever, when I step out of the cab and look up to see three—count 'em—three police cars with flashers swirling, crowded together in the space before the awning of my building. My muse—no fragile darling and generally startled into speech—is startled into silence as I run forward to investigate.

I have always, in these instances, an immediate assumption that whatever is happening has something to do with me which usually vanishes as common sense prevails. Common sense is prevailing when the doorman turns and sees me and shouts to the army of cops at the elevator, "Here she is."

I am surrounded by our men in blue and am between beginning to fear that Arthur is dead and becoming absolutely positive that Arthur is dead when one of them says,

"Are you Samantha Clementine?"

I'm positive. "Yes," I plead.

"Do you know a man who calls himself God?"

My mind snaps clear: The great beast falls . . . "Yes."

"Would you come with us please?"

"Of course," I say firmly: Falling and falling until this eye, this shattered eye . . .

I am in the back of the patrol car and off we zip, sirens blaring. I have never been in a police car before, let alone with sirens. It is fun.

"What's happened?" I call to the two men in front: dark-haired, heavy-bearded veterans both. This shattered eye has sprinkled on the grass.

The cop in the passenger seat calls back to me: "This guy God walked into a daycare center an hour ago with a high-powered rifle and started screaming. He's got two teachers and nineteen two and three-year-old kids in there, and he says he's gonna kill 'em if he doesn't talk to you."

The cop driving shouts back: "He says he's gonna kill 'em after he talks to you, too."

I think: Has sprinkled on the grass, yet nothing is in fragments that we knew . . . I think: Oh, shut up.

"You got my name through Lifeline?"

"Yeah," says passenger cop. Traffic is stopping for us and we are speeding across the 59th Street Bridge toward Queens with a cop car before us and one in back for escort. It is quite thrilling. "Hey," he says, "you're not Andy Clementine's wife, are you, in the D.A.'s office?"

"Yes," I shout. "Arthur."

"Yeah, right, Arthur," he says, and smirks at his partner who smirks back.

In my hyper-attuned state, I somehow understand this joke at once—with the same sense of excitement and clarity I felt when halfway through *The Ambassadors* I realized that Lambert Strether was so named because he was a proxy Christ and the two Mary's and his selfless mission and everything all fell into place and, anyway, the point is that if Arthur is Andy, Jones is Amos, and this is New York's finest's revenge for their work in indicting their grandma-killing confrère. When the thrill of revelation dies—fast—gloom descends: I am in hostile territory, among dangerous men. Arthur is traveling from meeting to meeting. Elizabeth is waiting in the airport for the three o'clock flight to Geneva. I am alone.

Belligerently, I jut my chin and think:

The great beast dies,
And vestal whores, their bare breasts lifted
To the holocaust skies,
Extend their arms

For the fragments of his body's empire,
And ceremonies will begin at noon
To obscure the faded thrill
Of his falling and falling.

This eye, this shattered eye,
Has sprinkled on the grass,
Yet nothing is in fragments that we knew,
And where his phallus fell,
There grows a naked tree,
And you and I, we scrambled to the top like
monkeys . . .

We are in Queens: I do not know where we are. All
Queens is divided into one part to me: two-family brick
houses with little yards and laundry fluttering on the lines
between one woman's daydreams and another's despair.
But then, we are on a Main Street, a long business district.
I am struck for some reason by a store that sells Indian
saris and home appliances. And then, we turn a corner,
and there are four million police cars, and policemen and
women in uniforms and plainclothes crouching behind the
cars, and many of them are pointing rifles at a little white
two-storied barracks across the street that has a large picture window on the second story, and a door on the first
with a rainbow painted on the sign above it and the words,
"Rainbow Daycare Center" in different colored letters.

Everything happens very fast. I get out of the car and
am whisked in a squadron of policemen toward a small
grocery store across the street from the center that is
apparently being used as command central. I see the faces
of women—the mothers—drawn and sorrowful, skim past
me. Then I have only time to feel the heaviness of fear sink
down on top of me as I pass close by all those guns: pistols
and rifles. There is something very substantial—un-
theoretical—weighty—and fatal—about a gun.

I am in the grocery store—swept through the door—
and a man is introducing himself as Captain Cerone. He is
short for a man, about two inches taller than me: a substantial piece of black suit with close-cropped hair and
worried eyes, and the scratchy jaw that seems to be a

requirement for joining the force. Something, come to think of it, about all these men—men everywhere—big, burly men—with guns no less—is beginning to make me feel very beardless.

I brace myself by checking on my poem: it is still there. The captain has me by the elbow and is guiding me with a sort of weary chivalry past the tomatoes and the dairy freezer to the deli counter behind which is the phone. He is giving me instructions but at this point I am in a daze—depressed, frightened, girlishly inadequate, frightened, teary, frightened, frightened—and can't make sense of them. Cerone is reassuring me and I hate him for it, but then he calls me Mrs. Clementine and I feel reassured. I try to think if I have heard any of his instructions: I remember I am not supposed to promise God anything and to keep him calm, but that sounds like the Old Testament to me. Then—too quickly, far too quickly—someone is putting the telephone receiver—and the lives of nineteen babies—into my hand.

I hold the phone to my ear. Someone guides me to a stool and I sit down behind the butcher's block. There are yellow legal-size papers scattered before me and a few pens. I eye the pens hungrily and lick my lips.

"Hello?" I say.

There is a long silence. I see men's faces intent all around me—bodiless, floating, judging. Then: "Sam?"

I feel myself relax at once. There is only the phone—the darkness of the phone and voices—there is only me and God. I am on familiar ground.

"God," I say, trying to take on my usual tone of control, "Sweetie, what are you doing?"

"Well," he says, "what I thought is I figured I'm going to first kill all these kids and these two teachers and then myself."

I fight off the urge to scream something sensible like "What?" and say: "Okay. Why are you going to do that?"

"It's just time," he says—and there is an authority, a self-assurance in his voice that I have never heard before. That and the fact that I do not hear any children crying in the background turn my heart into an anvil. "It's just time to stop all this nonsense," he says, "and do the job. She shouldn't have hurt me and the missiles and I'm going to stop it and bring it back."

Paralyzed, I'm brilliant. "You sound very upset," I say.

"No. The world's a daisy. Don't pull that Lifeline shit on me, Sam."

I do not apologize. We are battling for control of the situation, he and I, and I care about God, and if he wins, he loses.

"All right," I say, "then why do you want to talk to me?"

"Well, if you don't want to, hang up."

We both wait a bit, and then I say firmly: "Why do you want to talk to me?"

And another beat, more dangerous. If he answers my question, he cedes a little authority to me. I half expect to hear the shots go off. I sit there like a statue.

"I wanted to say goodbye," he says.

"I think maybe you want me to forgive you," I answer.

"I don't want to die alone, Samantha."

"I don't want you to die at all."

He yells—but it is a yell of anguish, which I take to be a good sign. He yells: "I can't! I can't! I have to! I have to!"

I don't know what this means—perhaps, in the stress of the situation, I have forgotten—and in the absence of an answer, I think: Brimstone vapors pluming from the gaping lips and curling through the canyons of the ear that lies there on its side . . .

"Sam?" he says softly.

Reflexively, I reach for a pen and begin to snap its point in and out with my thumb.

"Yes," I say.

"I think I have to go now," he says.

"I think the first thing we have to do," I say quickly, "is get those kids out of there."

He is silent.

"Okay?" I say. "They have nothing to do with this, God."

"Oh, Sam." His voice breaks. "I'm sorry. Forgive me, okay?"

"I'm your friend, God."

"You're my only friend."

"We have to get those children out of there before they get hurt."

He yells again, crying now: "That's all you care about. What is that, the fucking maternal instinct?"

"Well—" I say steadily, "do you think it's right to kill children?"

And I realize by the swiftness of his answer, by its tone of rehearsal, that this is what he's been waiting for, this is the crux of his self-justification. "It is when God does it," he says.

My own stupidity, and the petty pleasure he gets out of catching me up, makes me mad. "Damn it," I say, "I'm not so thrilled when He does it, and you're not God."

Cerone's eyes expand to the size of Frisbees and he gestures at me with both hands to calm down. To hell with Cerone.

But he's right. I have blown it. The situation falls apart in my hands like a mouldy rose. God starts ranting: "The rage of Marcodel released . . . The triumph of Death . . . Now is the moment . . ."

And, panicked, I am fighting to stop thinking: . . . the canyons of the ear that lies there on its side, have poisoned several of the parks, and yet the hideous thunders . . .

God has worked himself up to a fever pitch. Cerone's eyes are pleading with me. All around the grocery, men's eyes are turning to the picture window across the street, waiting, waiting . . .

"God," I shout, "stop this right now!"

He stops. The entire room is a held breath. We are all now waiting, our eyes on nothing, our ears pricking, waiting for the shots.

I take a big swallow. "Look," I say, "it's time to come out. Come out to me."

I hear God crying, fighting for air. "Why should I?"

"Because I'm your friend . . ."

"Oh yeah."

"And I love you. I'm your friend and I love you," and I am and I do, "that's why."

Grimly, finally, he answers: "I don't know you, Samantha."

"That's not true, God. That's not true and you know it isn't."

"I don't even know what you look like."

"Come out, then, and see."

"I don't even know what you look like."

"You know what I *am* like."

He screams, raging, crying: "I don't even know what you *look* like!"

I am about to describe myself when I am suddenly as sure as if it were the written thing that if I do, the massacre will begin.

Instead, I say, "If I show you, will you come out?"

And, like a sulky child, he answers: "Show me."

"Hold on," I say.

I put the phone on hold and set it down.

"What?" says Cerone.

I am staring at the paper on the butcher block, clicking the pen in and out in my hand. Should I write down what I have beforehand, just in case? Does it matter? When I have fears that I might cease to be . . .

Somebody calls quietly from further down the deli counter: "He wants her to go out there," and I realize, with a sense of violation, that someone else has been listening to the call.

"I have to show him my face," I tell Cerone.

"No," says Cerone.

"There is no no."

"There is no, and it's my no and it's no," says Cerone. "Talk to him some more."

I look up from the paper. "I can't reach him. He's gone beyond me. I have to show him my face."

"No," says Cerone.

"He's about to start," I tell him. "I know him. He's about to start. Methodically. Calmly. He's not even upset any-more. I could talk to him when he was upset. He's calm now—I calmed him down. Now, he's going to kill them."

Cerone turns to another plainclothesman. "Get them ready to go in."

I stand up.

"No," says Cerone.

"I won't talk to him anymore."

I look in his eyes. Damp, worried eyes. He is, I realize, a nice man. Somewhere behind the deli counter, I hear another man murmuring, talking to God, telling him to hold on, to wait for me. Cerone considers, shakes his head: "We'll talk to him." Then, apologetically: "Listen, Mrs. Clementine, you're the A.D.A.'s wife, you know?"

"Yes," I say, "I know. Believe me, I know whose wife I am. And if I don't show God my face, he's going to start— he's going to start any second."

We are studying each other—looking into each other's eyes—trying to find out everything about each other in the space of a second. But I am certain of only one thing: I have nothing more to say to God.

Then someone calls: "Captain, I think she's right. He's getting ready to blow."

Cerone takes a deep breath. Quietly, he says: "Okay. Tell him she's coming."

And it happens in a moment. Cerone has me by the elbow, he is marching me outside—mothers' faces, cars, cops' faces, guns—all are rushing past me.

"Step out in front of the blue car," Cerone is telling me. "I'm going to count to one and grab you."

I feel he is propelling me out there—as if I had not demanded it—against my will. Don't make me go, I am thinking. We are passing one car after another, and then there is the blue car coming closer and closer and beyond it the open street before the daycare center. We are there.

"I love Arthur," I say.

"I'll tell him," says Cerone.

And then I step out in front of the blue car, and I am standing about twenty yards from the center and the blank-faced picture window, and I am—I feel I am—I am sure I am—eyeball to eyeball with Marcodel.

Later, the reporters will ask me what I was thinking when I stood out there. When I stood out there for that one long moment, when finally, finally, my imagination grasped what I am, what this is, this Samantha, this temporary machine, this eternal consciousness a trigger-pull away from nothing. When, finally, I knew, if he shoots me,

I'll die; if a bullet the size of my thumb tears into me, I will
be sod and pavement. No clarity of soul appeared in that
moment to manifest its divergence from even the curling
of my pubic hair; no billion cells called out their indepen-
dent lives; no time proclaimed itself an illusion. Only this
one moment of Samantha arose with its possibilities for
every good thing. That was all. They will ask me what I was
thinking, and they will already have asked me the name of
my book of poems, and there will be TV cameras and
everyone will be waiting to write down what I say, and the
simple fact is: I will succumb. I will tell them I was thinking: I've got to do this for those kids.

I am thinking: *Here I am please don't kill me God here is my
face don't kill me please God here I am don't kill me don't kill me
God here's my face don't kill me* . . .

And then Cerone grabs me and pulls me back behind
the car.

I am, I guess, in shock. I am in a daze and my eyes feel as
if they have been propped open with crowbars as Cerone
marches me back past the startled gazes of the policemen
crouching everywhere.

Within seconds, the bright summer sun is ex-
tinguished—we are in the grocery again—and I am standing in front of the phone. I stare wildly at the phone. I
stare wildly at Cerone. Cerone's face and his collar are
drenched with sweat.

"Lady," he says, "you've got balls."

"Let's not discuss it," I say and pick up the phone.

I start to speak and then I glance down and see the pen
is still in my hand. And suddenly it all breaks loose, breaks
loose in its completeness, irresistible.

The phone to my ear, without saying a word, I begin
scribbling on the legal pad as fast as I can.

"Captain," someone calls, "He's not saying anything."

"What the hell are you writing?" Cerone asks me.

Helpless, I laugh.

Someone shouts: "Captain!"

Everyone—me included—glances up at the front of the
store. Across the street, we see two women peeking cautiously out of the day care center. Then, they step onto the

sidewalk and all at once, they are followed by a swarm of
toddlers in bright summer clothes. Chubby little boys and
girls with inquisitive faces are everywhere and their legs
are rising and falling clop-clop in a drunken march as they
waddle into the sunlight. I hear the cries of women nearby,
and men's shouts of thanksgiving. Then, policemen are
rushing forward to drag the babies out of the line of fire. I
am glad.

I continue writing:

The great beast falls
And vestal whores, their bare breasts lifted
To the holocaust skies
Extend their arms to catch
The fragments of his body's empire.
Ceremonies will begin at noon
To obscure the faded thrill
Of his falling and falling,
But still, we see:
This eye, this shattered eye
Has sprinkled on the grass,
Yet nothing is in fragments that we knew,
And where his phallus fell
There grows a naked tree—
How we scrambled to the top like monkeys!
Brimstone vapors pluming from the gaping lips
And curling through the canyons of the ear
That lies there on its side
Have poisoned several of the parks,
And yet the phlegmatic thunders
Of the legs falling and the arms falling
And the trunk severed at last by the vaginal incisors
Falling and falling
Did not make of our lake a fire:
We still are diving there as we did once,
Naked and white and clean of hair,
Nor have we forgotten the old men's stories
Of the child who drowned in the sludge at the bottom,
Nor have we ceased our seeking him,
Skimming over the bass-woven underweeds

As we watch ourselves from the tops of the branches,
Hearing the splashing and the laughter and the cries
Carried from where we play to where we play
On the bare bosom of the old spring breezes.

It does not seem very long, and I cannot tell yet whether
or not it is good. All of them seem good at first, but most of
them end up buried in the drawer. At any rate, I am free
of it. I am done scribbling by the time God comes out—a
tall, fat man in a gray sweatshirt stained with grease. A
long face with the jaw hanging open stupidly as the cops
frisk and handcuff him. Sad, idiotic eyes searching for me
over the top of a car, before they push him face down onto
the hood.

They would not let me talk with God before they processed him, except to assure him I'd be with him later,
which I did. He nodded dumbly, dazed. I don't think he
knew who I was.

After the press and a lot of thankful parents blessing
me, the cops drive me back to Manhattan, and I ask them
to drop me off at the Plaza so I can walk home. They tell
me they have been trying to reach Arthur and have finally
caught up with him in Brooklyn somewhere and he is on
his way which I am glad of because I figure I have a solid
two hours of hysterical tears coming to me.

I walk under the canopy of trees beside Central Park,
giving my purse a Lanskyesque check every now and again
to make sure my poem is still in it. I have just reached the
museum when I see a cab pull up in front of our apartment building and Arthur gets out. I cannot make out his
face where I am, but I can tell from his gestures that he is
harried and frazzled—he is worried about me. I cup my
hands to my mouth and give him a rebel yell.

Arthur turns, sees me—and runs out in front of a downtown bus, three crazed cab drivers and a stretch limo. They
miss him: this is my lucky day. I am running as fast as I can
past the museum toward him, already gearing up for my
well-earned tears.

Then Arthur is on my side of the street and he is

running toward me calling my name and I am running toward him, past the fountain, with my arms out and then—

Then—when we are about fifteen steps away from one another, a drop of water from the fountain flies twirling into the air between us, and I see it as it catches the sun, and I feel my body wash into it and I feel Arthur's body wash into it, too, and for a second, for a second in that drop of water spinning and flashing in the sun, there is nothing at all but the solid flow of my body into his and his into mine and ours into the body of everything, the solid, flowing, fleshly mass of everything forever. Just for a second, not even a second, except that there is no time, no time or space, just matter, matter forever, matter in love with itself, matter in love with itself eternally, and even when it is over, even though it is over in the very instant of infinity in which it began, I embrace my husband, finally, not in tears, but with a surge of crystal, pristine, perfect faith, thinking:

Come to me, come to me, Arthur. Come to me, all of you—all my darlings. I am Samantha Clementine, and it is going to be all right.

Trust me.

Trust me.